Shyt List

~~Be Careful Who You Cross~~

A Novel by
Reign

Library of Congress Control Number: 2007940465
ISBN: 0-9794931-1-0
ISBN 13: 978-0-9794931-1-9
Cover Design: Davida Baldwin www.oddballdsgn.com
Editor: Advance Editing Services
Graphics: Davida Baldwin
Typesetting: Davida Baldwin

First Edition
Printed in the United States of America

What up Folks,

Thanks for coppin' The Cartel Publications first street banger. The Cartel Publications promises to make sure we put out real shit. We strive to rep for all our folks who have to wake up, scratch, survive and sleep in the game day in and day out. Our stories may not be what all people wanna be faced with, but they are real and deserve to be told. If you continue to ride with The Cartel, we promise to ALWAYS ride for you. We appreciate your love and support and will continue to live up to your expectations.

In every book we drop, we promise to pay homage to Author's who kicked the door down on Street Lit. In this book, we give love to:

"K'WAN"

Kwan was one of the first authors to give street lit a name. We love you Brah and we preciate the love and real you put in your work. Keep grindin' on the top!!!

Also, I gotta shout out much love to, "The Cartel's Pep Squad". The squad is helping spread the word around about our novels! And we consider them, fam. Thanks ladies.

The Cartel Publications Pep Squad

Jessica aka "Lyric" (Squad Captain), Ms. Toya Daniels, Erica Taylor, Shawntress, Kim Gamble, Victoria "Tori" Johnson, Crystal and Lisa aka JSQueen625.

Charisse Washington
VP, The Cartel Publications

Dedication

I dedicate this book to every author who has tried to write a book without the backing. I know what its like. Stay on your grind. Good things come to those who grow tired of waiting. Take what's yours!

Acknowledgements

I'd like to thank T.Styles and Charisse Washington for giving me a chance. Its one thing to believe in a book, but it's a whole notha thing to put your money behind it. For that, I thank you both.

I'd also like to thank everyone who's reading this book now. Your support means a lot to me. If you like this one, you'll love my other novels coming to a bookstore near you.

I'd also like to thank my friends and my family members. You know who you are. Maybe one day I'll be accepted for who I am, and not what I do.

Chapter One

Hood Love At Its Best

The night summer air was hypnotic and a perfect breeze was blowing through and around the inner city buildings. 19 year old Yvonna's red Prada stilettos clicked quickly against the concrete pavement, leading toward her block.

She was irritated that the gum she was chewing had lost its flavor and that the thongs she was wearing had run so far up her ass, it was difficult to walk. She would've freed herself from the uncomfortable feeling but she was almost at her building in Southeast D.C. Not to mention her hands were occupied with grocery bags filled with food.

"You need help, shawty?!" yelled a neighborhood block head.

"Naw I'm good," she responded as she passed him walking seductively. She added a little extra in her step because she knew he was watching. "Boy, don't waste your time dreamin' bout it," she paused turning around to catch the lustful look in his eyes. "Cuz it's never gonna happen." She winked and continued her stroll to her apartment.

"Man ain't nobody payin' you no mind," he replied as he cupped his dick and balls. "Wit yo half crazy ass."

Crazy was a word she hated, and she contemplated smacking him for the disrespect, but thought better of it. Instead she shook her head and cut the corner of the fenced in entrance. She knew he wanted to fuck her just like the rest of the hustlers 'round her way.

As her mind wondered, she thought about Cream, one of her best girlfriends. She was mad at her for dropping her off two blocks from her building. If Cream hadn't fucked Yvonna's neighbor's husband, she would've been able to drop her off out front.

But Treyana swore that if she saw her anywhere near her block she'd stomp a mud hole in her ass. And with six brothers and sisters, Cream knew Treyana meant it. She didn't stop at just fucking him, she went as far as to shack up in a run down motel off of New York Avenue in D.C. with his bum ass. Best believe the dogs were called out on her, so Cream hid out.

When Yvonna reached the apartment building she shared with her 6 year old sister and as she would say, her senile veteran father, she managed to free three fingers to grab the building's door. Once inside she cracked it open, stuck her foot in to hold it steady and twirled her body inside. The glass door bounced on her ass once before she took two steps forward and allowed it to close fully behind her. She briefly placed the bags on the floor to catch her breath and looked up at the two flights of stairs she had to tackle before *finally* getting some rest.

"Damn! Maybe I should've let his ass help!" she said out loud.

Picking the bags back up, she forced herself up the dimly lit hallway. She smiled when she saw her door realizing in a minute she'd be able to get naked, sit on the couch and munch on the oatmeal crème pies she had in one of the bags.

Now upstairs, Yvonna placed the bags on the floor and reached for the keys in her pocket. Before letting herself in, she dug in her ass and adjusted the thong that had been holding her hostage for the past few minutes. She was so caught up in bullshit, that she hadn't heard or sensed the person in the dark hallway behind her.

"Don't scream," he whispered heavily in her ear as he placed his left hand firmly against her mouth. She could smell the faint scent of cocoa butter since his index finger was directly under her nose. "You fuckin' hear me?"

She nodded her head yes.

"Open the door."

It took her a minute to find the right key on the Burberry keychain. The sound of them jingling resonated in the hallway. When she located the key, she did as instructed and allowed him in as she wrestled with the bags.

"Hurry the fuck up!" he whispered again.

With the bags against the living room wall, they walked in and he locked the door behind them.

The apartment was totally dark with the exception of the light which illuminated from the huge fish tank against the living room wall. Just as she expected, her 6 year old sister Jesse was asleep and she saw no signs of her father.

With his hand still over her mouth he mumbled, "Now walk over to the couch! You betta not scream. You hear me?!"

She nodded yes. When she reached the couch, she bent over the edge as he demanded. With her ass in the air and her knees slightly bent, he reveled at her sexiness. The red Baby Phat shorts looked as if they were painted on. Still, they were in the way for what he had planned. With that, he tugged at them until they hung loosely at her ankles.

"Dayyyuummm!" he said focusing on her honey brown ass in the purple thongs. Then he ripped them off too. Yvonna squinted in pain because the thongs had rubbed her raw.

"Don't hurt me," she begged looking back at him. "I'll do any-thing you say just please don't hurt me."

"Didn't I tell you not to say shit?" He asked as he pressed up against her back to reach her ear. He placed more force on her than necessary.

She nodded yes.

"Then why da fuck you speakin'?" Sprinkles of spit touched her face.

She didn't respond.

"Don't say shit else!" He continued as he busied himself with the pussy he was about to take.

As he captured her silence, he entered her raw. His dick had grown a solid seven inches. He was so hard that if he'd been any harder, it would've felt like a bat going in and out of her tiny body. The veins on his dick were pulsating as he fucked her without remorse for how she felt. Licking his lips, he caught a brief glimpse of his balls slapping against her phat ass. When he realized he was being turned on even more, and on the verge of cum-ming before he wanted to, he allowed her ass cheeks to drop against his stomach. With one hand pressing on the small of her back to keep the arch, he grabbed her hair and used it as a reign to ride her from behind.

"Shit!! I'm bout to cum!" He moaned. He had her in the per-fect position and could no longer hold out.

Hearing this, Yvonna decided there was no way she was about to be left hanging. She slyly backed up into him and twirled her hips with each motion he made. But when she did, he was brought closer to his point.

"I'm about to cummm! Shit!!!!" He yelled.

"Shhhhhh!" She managed thinking her little sister may over-hear them.

"Fuck that," he responded. "Your pussy shouldn't be so good."

Yvonna didn't care what he did now because while he was yap-ping off at the mouth, she'd already gushed her wetness all over his dick. Unlike him she was able to moan hers out giving off the impression that she hadn't cum.

"Stay right there." He informed. "Don't move!"

When he took his slippery dick out, and aimed for her back to release his cum, it reached the glass coffee table instead. Yvonna burst out into laughter seeing the mess he'd made. He chuckled and fell into her, his cold platinum diamond chain pressed against her skin.

"You know you crazy right?" He asked out of breath.

"I'm crazy? How you figure?"

"Cuz you stay likin' this rough shit." He replied before pulling up his True Religion jeans. He then disappeared into the darkness of the apartment and returned with a warm washcloth.

"And you love that I like it rough. Anyway, I thought you couldn't come over tonight," she responded as she rose so he could clean both of their wetness from her body. When he rubbed her exposed vagina with the washcloth, she tensed up due to the raw-ness she felt. On the sly, he stuck his finger inside of her.

"Damn! You still wet! Let me hit it again real quick!" he

Reign

reached for himself.

"Stop boy!" She snatched the washcloth from him and cleaned the mess off the table. "I'm already in pain messin' wit yo silly ass!" She slid back into her shorts leaving the zipper opened so her tiny belly could breathe. She didn't see her panties and wasn't searching for them either. She flipped on the kitchen light. "And put them groceries on the counter," she continued as her tiny feet slapped against the cold hardwood floor. "Might as well make yourself useful."

Yvonna wondered why he popped up the way that he did. "I thought you were goin' to the party tonight." She grabbed the black rubber hair band that she kept on her arm, and pulled her hair into a ponytail which sat on the top of her head. "You act like you ain't have no time for me earlier when I called."

"I always got time for you." he pinched her ass.

"Move, boy!" she yelled secretly loving his aggression. "And how you know what time I was gonna be home?"

"I waited on you. Plus you always go to the store at night. You betta switch your routine up."

"I ain't changin' shit! I hate waitin' in dem long ass lines. At night I'm in and out. And don't try to skip the subject B. What's up wit the party?"

"I'm still goin'." He placed the bags on the counter and looked as if he had something on his mind. "I just came to check you before I left. Plus I wanna talk to you about somethin'."

"Everything okay? Besides the fact that you're standin' me up for the movies again?"

"I'll make it up to you shawty."

"Oh I know that," she said curling her lips. "But you betta know it too!"

He walked up behind her and placed his arms around her waist. The diamond studded belly ring she wore scratched his arm lightly.

"So you really gonna do it huh?"

"Yes, Bilal," she responded stealing a piece of his apple that he'd taken from the grocery bag. She already knew what he was talking about. Her transporting drugs from D.C., to New York for the gang he belonged to. "And don't start with me because I don't want to hear it."

"What if I tell you I don't want you doin' it? Then what?"

"We already talked about this Lal!"

"I know we talked about it," he said as a look of concern overtook him. "But I don't think you should do it. Once you get involved in this shit you stuck."

Yvonna stopped what she was doing and looked into his eyes. His long eyelashes added softness to his rugged features. His black and Spanish heritage made him look exotic. And because he stayed in the streets, the sun caused his skin to bronze.

Everything about him was perfect to hear Yvonna tell it. From his 6'2 inch height, to his large dick. And no matter how much he loved wearing plain white T's, baggy jeans and Nike boots, he still looked like a model with a thuggish quality. He was tatted up. His favorite was the one on his arm which read "LalVon" inside of a coffin. It represented his motto that it would be he and Yvonna till death.

"I hear you, Bilal," she smiled walking over to him before stealing a passionate kiss. She then ran her hand over his silky goatee. "But I'm a big girl and I been wantin' to get with the Young Black Millionarz before I met you in high school. You act like I'm an angel or somethin'."

"Oh I know you be throwin' them bows." He chuckled. "That's one of the reasons I love you." He looked into her hazel brown eyes.

"But shit has changed with the YBM. It ain't how it use to be. Ever since Crazy Dave and his step brother Swoopes got put on, niggas been lunchin' out. Some dudes doin' stuff we ain't use to do. Like stickin' up mothafuckas and shit. They got the game all fucked up."

"Why they even let them in?" she questioned.

"Because they thorough and don't give a fuck," he advised. "And you need a few niggas like that on the squad."

"I don't know 'bout Swoopes but I think Dave's a punk for real for real." Yvonna said fanning her hand in the air. She hated his fucking guts. "Plus I don't appreciate him telling people Sabrina's pussy smelled like cat piss. It ain't like he fucked her so how would he know anyway?"

"How you know he ain't hit?"

"I *don't* know." She removed the black shirt she was wearing and allowed her titties to show. She hated clothes. "But he don't eitha."

"No lie, your girl do need a lesson in hygiene." he laughed pinching her nipples.

"And how do you know?" She hit him on the hand. "Don't be talkin' about her. That's my friend!"

"Everybody know that girl's pussy stink! Every time she get out a car, niggas turn the other way. I mean she a big girl and all, but she still can wash her ass. That's ree-dic-culous!"

Yvonna couldn't say much because although she was one of her best friends, she knew what Bilal was saying was true. On many occasions she pulled her to the side to have a conversation with her about her odor and she still couldn't get it right. Most women wouldn't have the heart to tell their friends but Yvonna did. She felt sorry for the nigga that fucked and got her pregnant.

They were still talking when Bilal's cell phone rang.

"Hello," he said walking away from her. He looked back to see if she was watching. She was. "I can't hear you." He said as he walked further away. He was trying to space himself away from Yvonna since she was always sweating him about his calls.

Yvonna picking up on the cue walked back into the kitchen. *Why the fuck he got to go in the other room?* She thought. *I hope he ain't fuckin around on me again!*

Bilal was a good dude but just like most, he made the mistake of stepping out on her every now and again. And ever since the last time, Yvonna didn't trust him. It didn't make her feel any better that he wasn't with the Young Black Millionarz right now, and he was at her house. It didn't help that he slept over there almost every night despite living on the Maryland side of town. Once a cheat always a cheat in her book. Still, love wouldn't allow her to leave him alone.

"Who dat?" she asked walking up to him while he was in the living room on the couch. She could no longer bite her tongue.

"I'ma hit you lada man." he said as he ended the call. He didn't want her going off like she had many times in the past. Yvonna had a temper so bad that when she got angry, she would get violent and not remember doing it.

"Bilal, who the fuck was that?!" She yelled as she took the black New York Yankees cap off his head and hit him with it.

"Stop trippin girl!"

"Don't tell me to stop trippin!" she yelled as she snatched the Blackberry off his hip and hit send to connect to the last caller. Bilal tried to get a hold of her but she was too quick. When the phone rang and someone answered she asked, "Who's this?"

"Why you got his phone?" When she realized it was a *he*, suddenly she felt stupid for violating Bilal's privacy.

"Oh…," she said feeling slightly dumb. "It's *just* you."

"Yeah it's me," Dave responded irritated. "Why you bein' pressed?"

"Give me my phone girl," Bilal said snatching the blackberry from her. "How you feel now? Stupid?"

Silence.

"Hello," Bilal said placing the phone back on his ear.

"You gotta get your girl in check man. She can't be goin' through your shit."

"Don't worry about me, partna!" he smiled. "I got this over here."

"No you don't!" Yvonna yelled still up in his biz.

"I hope you're not serious about what you gonna do either." Crazy Dave said reminding him of their last conversation. "Real niggas don't go out like that."

"I *am* serious, and just cuz I know what I want, don't mean I'm not real."

"Yeah aight, man," he laughed. "You betta hope she don't find out, cuz marrying her ain't gonna change the fact that shawty on the way."

Bilal looked at Yvonna hoping she couldn't hear what Dave said.

"Like I said, let me do me and you do you."

"Yeah whateva. Don't forget 'bout dem dudes neitha. Swoopes owe a lot of money to some cats and that'll be enough to settle all debts."

"I told ya'll I ain"t wit that shit." He was mad he brought it up.

"Nigga, ain't nobody sayin' you got to do shit." Dave felt Bilal was being soft and his voice was as deep as Method Man's when he addressed him. "But you the only one they trust. You get em to the club and me and Swoopes will do the rest."

"What I tell you 'bout talkin' 'bout this shit over the phone?"

"Yeah whateva, nigga," Dave replied. "Just don't try and back out."

After he hung up, Bilal placed his phone in his pocket instead of the clip. He had a few females lingering around that he hadn't fucked in awhile but nothing serious. Sitting down on the couch, he removed his boots as if nothing happened.

"Where my slippers ma?"

"Fuck dem slippers," she frowned. "What his hatin' ass say cause I know he was talkin' bout me?" She plopped on the couch next to him and his hand fondled her breasts. "You know he wanna fuck me right?"

"Did he tell you that shit?" he asked like he was on his way to confront him. Sitting up straight he awaited her answer.

"No…I can just tell. Whenever he come around he got to say somethin' to me, even if I ain't speakin' to him."

"You be on his shit too. Don't get dude fucked up. Dave ain't tryin' to get at you, he just not use to girls speakin' their minds. But I'ma need you to stop clockin' my calls Yvonna. That shit ain't cool no more. We ain't kids."

"Fuck that!" Yvonna said slapping his hands off of her. "You just betta not be cheatin' again, Bilal. Cuz dis time I'm leavin' you!"

"Stop comin' for my head 'bout dat cheatin' shit! You know I ain't fuckin' over you no more."

"Well you did! You fucked me up cuz I would've never thought you'd step out on me."

Bilal sighed. Once a week he had to prove to her he was a changed man.

"I don't wanna to talk 'bout that shit no more, Yvonna! You can't be monitorin' my phone calls and shit. It's bad for bizness."

"As long as we're together," she responded reaching for his phone only to realize it wasn't on his hip. "Nothing's off limit."

With that she went for his pockets. He didn't fight and instead of grabbing his phone, she felt a tiny velvet box. Pulling it out her eyes got as big as saucers. When she opened it, a diamond solitaire ring stared at her. Without waiting, Bilal got on one knee as she began to fan herself anxiously with her hands.

Taking the box from her he said, "Yvonna, I fuck wit…I mean," he paused clearing his throat and trying to avoid using slang. "I love you. You're the only shawty I can see spendin' the rest of my life with. And I'm bein' real when I say that. I can have fun wit you, ride or die wit you and most of all, I can see havin' kids wit you. There's nobody out here for me but you."

"Bilal I can't believe-,"

"Don't say nothin', baby," He said rubbing the tears from her eyes. "When I see how you look afta your sister despite your father being fucked up I smile because I know you would hold me down if shit got rough. We got each otha, and that's real. I don't care what people say bout you, or bout us bein' together. Everything I do is for you. You a dime, Yvonna. You fuck me like I like to be fucked. You can cook your ass off, and you understand the game I'm in and respect it. Fuck dem hatin' mothafuckas out there! I know what I want and what I want for the rest of my life is you. So what I'm askin' you, baby is…will you do me the honor of being my wife?"

Yvonna jumped up and down and kissed him on every inch of his face before she mumbled what appeared to be a yes. As she thought about their new life together, she also thought about all the bullshit she went through to get to this point. The cheating, the late night calls on his cell phone and the nights she went looking for him only to find him with another girl.

Bilal stayed fucking around on her in the beginning, but no matter what, he always let it be known that he wasn't leaving her for another bitch. There were females who tried to get him to change his mind, and one in particular took it all the way by telling Yvonna. Bilal was known as a "Ruthless Mothafucka" with manners. He took it as far as it needed to be took and no farther. If he was coming for you, you'd know why and that was a turn on for a lot of the chicken heads around the neighborhood.

After Yvonna fucked up the female who told her about Bilal, she approached him about it. And instead of him being a punk, he manned up and told her the truth. But Yvonna wasn't a slouch and she didn't forgive easily. For six months she cut his ass off. She drove him crazy not accepting his calls or visits. Little did he know, she was hurting as much as he was. But she decided that she wouldn't take him back until she made him sweat.

That's when she started dating this nigga name Lucy. He was known around the way for being a player. She had the neighborhood buzzing when word got out that the *LL Cool J* look a like wanted to give up everything for Yvonna. When Bilal found out he stepped to them both at Jasper's restaurant. Because Lucy wasn't no busta ass nigga, Yvonna knew that Bilal was ready for war and most of all, ready to die for her. At that time she missed him so much that she stopped the games and walked out with Bilal leaving Lucy behind.

"So what up, ma?" he responded as she continued to bombard him with kisses. "You gonna marry me or what?"

"Yes! Yes! Yes! You know I'ma fuckin' marry you!"

"I wanna tell your father," he said standing up moving to the room. In all this time he never got to meet him. "I need his blessings."

"NO!" she jumped up. "He'll find out soon enough."

"Why you don't want me to meet the man? We been kickin' it for three years and you *still* don't want me to meet him. Why?"

"You marryin' *me* so that's all that matters," she said kissing him again. She *really* didn't want her father embarrassing her. Ever since he'd been back from the war, he hadn't been the same.

11

Needless to say Bilal didn't leave her that night. Like always, they crawled in the bed Yvonna shared with her six year old sister Jesse. One of the things Yvonna hated about the apartment was not having her own space. But she knew Jesse was just as frustrated.

Needing a bigger place was one of the main reasons Yvonna wanted to get with YBM. She needed the cash to get she and Jesse out of the two bedroom apartment and into something bigger, without her father. But now it looked as if the three of them would be a happy family.

"I love you." Yvonna said as she lay on her side, and turned her head to kiss Bilal who was behind her holding her tight.

"I love you too, ma."

When she looked at Jesse she smiled when she saw her sleeping heavily in front of her. She thanked God for finally bringing her closer to something she always wanted, a family of her own. What she didn't say out loud was that something told her that the happiness wouldn't last.

Chapter Two

A Tough Awakening

The Crimson colored liquid pressed heavily against Yvonna's eyelids. "Why would you kill Bilal daddy?!" she cried as she stared at him while he stood near the front door. "And you hurt Jesse too!"

One minute Yvonna was sleep and the next minute she was looking at Bilal lying beside her, with his head blown completely from his body. To make matters worse, she turned to her left and saw her baby sister Jesse convulsing and loosing a lot of blood. He had shot both of them at close range. And although Jesse was alive, she was pulling for air.

"I'm sorry Yvonna," he said softly, as she watched his glazed over hazel eyes. "I thought he was an intruder."

"I hate you! I fuckin' hate you! If Jesse dies I'll kill you myself!" she yelled as she ran to the phone to call the ambulance.

And when she turned around to confront him again, he was gone. She didn't give a fuck. All she cared about was saving Jesse. The operator could barely understand her because she was hysterical as she provided details.

"He killed my boyfriend and shot my sister! Please help!" she finally managed.

"I'm sending someone now, mam. Stay calm." The operator said.

When they finally arrived and Yvonna saw the trucks pull up in front of her building, she felt faint. What was to become of her life now? She gave the police the only information she had about her father but it was no good. She hated him! She hated even being a part of him. After all he did, she prayed the police would find him to take him away.

All she wanted was for Jesse to get well. That was her only wish. Sliding into the ambulance, she smiled at Jesse when she saw she was still conscious. But when she reached for Jesse's hand, she pulled away. Yvonna was hurt but figured Jesse blamed her for not being able to stop her father sooner. And as far as she was concerned, it was her fault.

As the paramedics gave Jesse oxygen and checked her vitals, Yvonna broke down crying. She knew nothing about her life would be the same, and she was right.

Chapter Three

Hood Disaster

The sound of tennis shoes scuffing against the filthy floor, crying and hysteria filled the busy hospital.

"I'm soo sorry, Yvonna." Sabrina said hugging her tightly. Her pregnant belly acting as a barrier between them. "Damn! Why the fuck Bilal have to die?!"

"I don't know. This is a fuckin' nightmare!" Yvonna cried. "And what about my sister? I'll kill myself if she dies!"

"She gonna be aight. At least she made it."

Sabrina wearing a pair of jeans, and a white t-shirt that said "Big and Beautiful" looked very uncomfortable in her clothes. Her red dreds were tied up in a ponytail and she was doing her best to console Yvonna despite being upset. You would've thought he was her man.

Cream was also by Yvonna's side, offering as much support as possible considering she didn't know what to say at a time like this. Wearing a pair of grey sweatpants which she filled out perfectly with her phat round ass, she had a body like Beyonce. The plain white t-shirt she wore exposed her flat stomach and sexy physique.

"Why the fuck did this have to happen to me? He was gonna marry me ya'll!" she advised showing them her ring. "Now he gone!"

They both stared at the ring in shock. They knew full well Bilal was not the type of dude to get married, even if it was to Yvonna.

"I'm so sorry, Yvonna." Cream said gripping her hand tightly. Every finger on Cream's hand was covered with a ring.

"Bilal gone ya'll!" Yvonna continued saying the same thing. "My sister's laying upstairs in a hospital bed and its all father's fault! Why, Brina?! Why he leave me to deal wit dis shit on my own?!"

"I don't know," Sabrina said as she maintained the one arm hold she had on her. Yvonna's face was pressed against her left breast. "You know he ain't neva been shit. I've never seen that man since I've known you. It's like you've always handled shit on your own. Why should this time be any different?"

When they heard what sounded like arguing in the background, they looked behind them to see Crazy Dave attempting to calm Swoopes down. Dave's back was faced the girls so they couldn't see what he was saying, or hear either of them clearly over the hospital noise. But Swoope's evil facial expressions were enough.

"Hold fast!" Crazy Dave advised with his hands up. "Let me find out what went down before we start kickin' up shit!"

"Find out what went down?" Swoopes repeated as he glared at Yvonna with disgust. "I don't believe shit that bitch say out her mothafuckin' mouth! You know she crazy!"

Swoopes grunted because he wanted to unleash four hot slugs into Yvonna's head. Bilal's death meant he couldn't carry out the YBM's plan to rob, Rock and Diamond Wayne from New York, two dealers who were coming in town for the weekend on business.

Bilal scheduled a meeting to buy some weight from them and the YBM members would be in the background ready to rob them. But with him dead, the plan would not go down. And with Swoopes owing some other dealers fifty thousand dollars, his life and the life of his family members were in danger.

"So what you wanna do? Go over there and blast her head off with a thousand witnesses watchin? With all the noise you makin' right now if somethin' *did* happen to the bitch, who you think they gonna remember?"

Swoopes remained quiet when he looked around and saw several people watching.

"That's what da fuck I thought! Now, let me find out what's goin' on!"

"Yeah aight!" Swoopes responded angrily. He had so much hate in his heart you couldn't come within twelve feet of him without feeling it. "Let me get out of here before I choke that bitch."

When Yvonna saw him leave, she sat up straight. Dave took a deep breath and walked over toward them.

"You aight, shawty?" He asked Yvonna as he pulled his cap down and sat in the available seat next to Cream.

"Not really," she said wiping the tears from her face.

"Jesse don't look too good." Cream advised him, still holding Yvonna's hand. "They don't know if she gonna make it." He looked over at Sabrina who was silently crying.

"You aight girl?" he asked Sabrina.

"Naw…too much is happenin' in one night!"

"Shit!" he said as he placed his face in his hands and looked over at Yvonna again. "Listen, I know you don't fuck wit me, but Bilal was my nigga. So if you need anything let me know. I'm not gonna get into your head 'bout what happened. We got plenty of time for that later."

Yvonna didn't say much. It wasn't a secret that she couldn't stand him. When she hoarded his ass by not even responding, he stood up, placed his hand on Yvonna's shoulder, and said "I'll be in touch." Like a threat instead of a promise. With that he walked off leaving them alone.

"I can't stand that mothafucka!" Yvonna responded as she took her feet out of Bilal's slippers. Pulling her knees toward her chest, she gripped her legs tightly.

"I know," Cream replied. "But he sounded like he was really worried about you."

"Fuck him!" Yvonna spat. "The only person he cares about is his mothafuckin' self. He ain't neva want me and Bilal to be together in the first place."

"I don't want you worryin' 'bout him." Sabrina responded bringing her closer to her big fleshy body, causing her feet to fall on the floor again. "You got us, and that's all that matters."

17

Yvonna fell into her hug. She realized that if her sister died, what Sabrina was saying would be true. Outside of Sabrina and Cream she didn't have anybody in her life that she really fucked with. Her closest friend Gabriella disappeared off the face of the earth when she was younger and she was the only one who Yvonna felt really cared about her. It didn't matter that whenever she was around Gabriella, she stayed in trouble.

And her aunt Jhane' on her mother's side, didn't want to have anything to do with Yvonna. The only person Jhane' was concerned about was Jesse.

Thirty minutes later Jhane rushed into the hospital to speak to the doctors. When Yvonna stood up to greet her, Jhane looked at her coldly.

"Get the fuck away from me, bitch!" Jhane told her with her fist balled up. "When Jesse pulls through, she's staying with me. I don't care what you or that deadbeat father of yours says." She walked off to talk to the doctors.

"Don't worry about her." Sabrina gripped her.

"Yeah! She's just upset at what's happening with Jesse." Cream added.

Yvonna didn't want to say anything, but Jhane's attitude toward her hurt but she was going to play it off. *Fuck my family.* She thought. *I got my girls and they got me! And when my sister gets betta, the three of dem will be all I care about.*

But little did she know, her statement was hardly true.

Chapter Four

Buried

Side conversations danced throughout the home as people tried to be friendly considering a funeral had taken place.

"You're like a daughter to me." Mrs. Santana said to Yvonna as she hugged her at Bilal's wake.

"I thought you would hate me," Yvonna cried.

"No…this isn't your fault, Yvonna. It's your father's."

"I hope you can forgive me." Her tears stained the grey silk blouse she wore underneath her jacket. "I don't know how I'm gonna go on without Lal!"

"You can't worry about that anymore sweetheart." she said taking a deep breath. "We have to pull ourselves together and move on with our lives. Because if I don't," Mrs. Santana said wiping her black thick hair from her face. "I don't know what I'll do."

Bernice Santana was a hustler's mother in every sense of the word. Unlike some mothers who steered their sons away from hustling, she introduced him to it. His father, Dylan, was a drug dealer who died by the hands of his own best friend, Tree. But what many people didn't know was it was Bernice who helped him. He knew the only thing Bernice gave a fuck about was money. So he made her an offer she couldn't refuse, forty percent of the money he'd take from Dylan.

So Bernice arranged for Dylan to meet her at an empty warehouse, and when he got there, Tree forced him to take him to the money and weight he had hidden in a secret location. When they found it, they murdered him and burned his body in an abandoned car.

Years later, Tree was indicted on King Pin charges and Bernice managed to convince him that her fourteen year old son Bilal was ready to take things over. In lust with her, Tree told her where to find his connect, and how to get a hold of some money he had tucked away. She assured him she'd never leave his side, and would make sure his books were straight.

Bilal quickly proved he was a natural born hustler. And when his business was up and running, Bernice left Tree to rot in prison by no longer accepting his calls or going to visit. Tree promised to pay her back but she moved around so much, he could never find her. He was still looking for her to this day.

"Stop crying Yvonna." Bernice said wiping her face with her fingers covered in diamonds. "Please."

"Okay." She sniffled. "I'll try."

Yvonna tried to be strong because she could tell Mrs. Santana was trying to save face in front of everyone. And if Yvonna persisted in making her feel like *she* felt, she knew Bernice wouldn't be able to compose herself.

Just then Cream and Sabrina walked over to them. Cream looked tasteful in the black one piece Sean Jean dress she chose to wear along with Treyana's husband Avante on her arm. Cream's fire red hair was pinned up in a bun and for a second, nobody wondered why Avante chose her over Treyana's big mouth dusty ass. When she first stole Avante everyone was shocked because the way she ran behind Yvonna, they assumed she was gay.

Sabrina was right beside them wearing black pants and a red top. Her cheeks were dark on the sides which were typical of most obese women. Her arms were out exposing the dark spots that before she gained one hundred pounds, visibly showed her elbows. But despite how big she was, Sabrina was still very attractive. Her smile appealed to everyone the moment you saw it. She softened her features with the natural red locks that fell on her shoulders.

Sabrina and Cream gave Mrs. Santana a hug. "I'm so sorry about your loss." Cream said as Avante offered his condolences too. Avante favored Tyrese greatly.

"Thank you baby," she smiled lightly. "I'll be alright."

"You okay Yvonna?" Cream asked rubbing her gently on the back. "Can I do anything for you?"

"I'm good," she lied. "Thanks anyway."

"You want anything to eat?" Sabrina asked Mrs. Santana as she held on to her own plate with one hand and her nine month pregnant belly with the other.

"No," she smiled rubbing Sabrina's belly. "I should be waiting on you. You look like you're about to bust any day now."

Sabrina smiled.

"I'm fine. Thanks though."

After everyone talked about the man Bilal was, Yvonna broke away to prevent from spoiling everyone's mood. Hearing his name over and over panged her heart. Plus she needed to check on the condition of her sister who was stabilized but still in the hospital. After they told her she was okay over the phone, she ran into Dave who was wearing a pair of jeans and a white t-shirt.

"Look what I got." he said showing her his tattoo. "That was my nigga. Know what I mean?"

Yvonna glanced down at his tattoo and saw *Bilal, rest in peace homie* tatted on his arm.

"That's nice." Yvonna said trying to be hospitable considering how she felt about him. "When you have time to do that?"

"Yesterday."

"Well I'm sure he'd appreciate you showin' love like that but if you'll excuse me."

"Hold up," he said grabbing her arm. "When you gonna tell me what *really* happened?"

She couldn't believe Dave was asking her about details at a time like this. She wasn't even thinking about talking about the murder. She looked up at his face for any signs of *real* sorrow. What she saw was his red eyes and knew immediately he was high.

Crazy Dave was handsome but mental. He looked like Young Buck without the cornrows. He was known for doing crimes without thinking things through. He was the man you went to when you wanted things done *illegally*. Although he used his rep as a means to get what he wanted, nobody knew that everything he did was to fit in.

Standing 6'1 inches tall, he was ripped. If he wasn't so unpredictable, he would've made somebody a good catch. But taming him was out of the question because he listened to no one.

"I don't want to talk about that right now."

"Well you betta be tellin' me somethin'." He grabbed her arm again. "Because from what I'm hearing, shit don't add up."

"Like I said," she said snatching away from him. "I don't want to talk about it."

Dave frowned and said, "You know some of the niggas from the YBM wanted me to take you out right?"

"Who? Swoopes? I know about the niggas he owe. Tell him don't try to put that shit on me."

He squeezed his chin and approached her. "Bilal was supposed to help us get some serious dough. So his murder hurt. Now because he was my man, I told them to leave you alone."

"Bilal's dead and that's all ya'll care about? Money?"

"Like I said, it's because of me you're still alive. And I'm not sure how much longer I can hold them off. They wanna know what happened, and so do I."

"I told everybody what happened, Dave! I loved him and I hope you not saying I'd hurt him! He was the only person who gave a fuck about me. If they want to be mad at somebody tell them to be mad at my father. He's the one who pulled the trigger! I'm outta here!" she stormed off.

Leaving him alone.

Chapter Five

Do What You Do

Jerry Springer's voice resonated throughout the hospital room. "I don't know where he is! The only thing I'm concerned about is Jesse." she responded to the detective while focusing on the television set.

"Okay, Ms. Harris," Detective Lily said. "But if you hear from him, tell him we need to speak to him immediately. If he's as sick as you say he is, we can help him."

"Like I said," she responded lowering her voice so that her sister, who still hadn't regained consciousness, wouldn't be disturbed. "If I hear from Joe," she said referring to her father. "I'll call you!"

When Yvonna slammed her cell phone shut, she gently touched her sister's hand. She couldn't imagine how Jesse would react having her arm amputated.

As she looked at her face, she wondered if the fire their mother died in three years earlier was an accident or if her father had something to do with it too. Her mother Diana died on Christmas day and Yvonna *still* hated the holiday. Even before her father's sickness caused by the Vietnam war, he was a dishonest man. He wasn't even living in the home when he showed up out the blue that fateful day.

The last thing Yvonna remembered after her father showed up, was her mother's corpse being taken out of the house, and the cops drilling her about what happened. To prevent being separated from her sister, she told them it was an accident caused by a candle. The house had been burned so badly, they took her word for it.

Brushing her soft brown hair in a ponytail, she slid into Bilal's slippers and walked outside of Jesse's hospital room to the vending machine. It had been two days since she'd eaten. She hoped she'd be able to keep something down now since everything she ate came up.

The moment she got off the elevator, she was surprised to run into Cream. She was wearing grey sweatpants and a pink Baby Phat t-shirt no bra. Yvonna had called her earlier to give her Jesse's room number but she didn't answer the phone.

"Cream?" Cream turned around with a shocked look on her face.

"Oh…uh…hey, Yvonna. How's Jesse?"

"She's doin' betta. She still don't know 'bout her arm though. They got her doped up so she's totally numb. I just hope she wakes up while I'm here."

"Damn." She looked at the floor and it became apparent that she was trying to think of something to say. "Did she get my roses?"

"Yeah they came today. She's in room 267 if you wanna go up and see her. I was just comin' to get somethin' to munch on right quick."

"Oh I'll be up later." She turned around to walk away.

"Is everything okay?" Yvonna called out to her.

"Uh…yeah," she responded turning around. "I'll see her in a little while."

"Isn't' that why you're here?"

"Huh?"

"Cream," Yvonna laughed. "What's wrong wit you? You're actin' like you're trying to hide somethin'."

"I'm not."

"So you're lying to me now?" Yvonna asked lowering her voice.

"Please don't put me in the middle of this, Yvonna," she blurted out. "I'm both of ya'll's friends."

"Girl, what are you talkin' about? Put you in the middle of what?" Yvonna asked now intrigued by her shift in mood. Any other time she'd be all up her ass but now she was avoiding her like she was contagious.

With that Cream handed her a greeting card she had in the bag she was carrying. When Yvonna pulled it out, it read, *Congratulations on your new bundle of joy!* She put the card back in the bag and her frown was replaced with a huge smile.

"She had the baby?!" Yvonna yelled holding her mouth. Cream nodded yes. "Oh my Gawwd! Why didn't she tell me? Take me to her room. I wanna see her."

Cream did as she was told although it was obvious she didn't want to. Yvonna was so caught up in the good news that she didn't notice.

When they reached the room, Yvonna was surprised by everyone who was there. Sabrina sat up in the bed when she saw Yvonna enter, before looking at Cream like she wanted to rip her eyes out. But it was who was at her bedside that had Yvonna puzzled. Mrs. Santana was holding the brand new baby boy, and cooing like a proud parent. Dave was also there with Swoopes, and two other dudes from the YBM.

"Why do I get the impression that I wasn't invited on purpose?" she questioned as she entered the room and looked at everyone. No one mumbled a word.

"So you had the baby huh?" she asked as she walked over to Mrs. Santana and reached out for him. Mrs. Santana looked at Sabrina and when she nodded that it was okay, she reluctantly handed the baby over. "Hey, cutie." she sang. "Welcome to the world. I'm your auntie Yvonna and I'm gonna spoil you rotten." she kissed him on the cheek.

Despite the connection she was building with the baby, the room was still shockingly quiet.

"I have to talk to you, Yvonna," Sabrina said. "In private."

On queue Mrs. Santana got up and carefully took the baby from Yvonna who wasn't ready to let him go.

"Let me give him back to the nurse. It's time for his feeding."

"Okay," Sabrina smiled. "Can everybody leave us alone please?"

Swoopes walked toward the door with the other YBM members. *"I'ma get yo ass."* He mouthed so only she could see him.

"Fuck you." She responded back.

When everyone left Mrs. Santana turned around and said, "Are you sure you don't want me to come back after I take the baby to the nursery?"

"No…I'll be fine. I need to do this alone."

Something was wrong. And Yvonna sat in the chair looking at Sabrina praying she wouldn't say anything that would cause her more pain. She knew the moment she talked to Cream that something was up, and now she was going to find out what.

Before this secret, she and Sabrina were the best of friends. And her apprehensiveness hurt.

"What's going on, Sabrina?" she questioned as the faint scent of rotten pussy filled the room. *Even now she can't wash her ass.* Yvonna thought.

"Before I say anything I wanted you to know that I love you. You know that right?"

"I hope so, Sabrina. So stop beatin' around the bush and tell me what's up!"

"I'm tryin' to, Yvonna," she responded looking down at the eggshell colored comforter that covered her bed. "It's just that what I'm about to tell you, might fuck up our friendship and I don't want it to. You like a sister to me."

Yvonna listened attentively and pulled the grey New York hoodie tightly together sensing a chill coming on.

"Okay," Yvonna responded her voice quivering. "I'm ready for you to tell me the deal."

"I just had Bilal's baby."

"You…w…what?" she leaned in to be sure she heard her correctly. "Can you say that again cuz I thought you said somethin' else."

"I said," she swallowed. "That I was pregnant by Bilal."

Now she realized she *did* hear her correctly. "How you tellin' me you had Bilal's baby, Sabrina? Huh?" The room was spinning causing her to feel a little off balance. She placed her hand on

Sabrina's bed for support. "I'm not understandin' what you sayin' right now."

"Please listen-,"

"Fuck that shit Sabrina!" Tears escaped her eyes by the pounds. That would explain why everyone reacted the way that they did when she entered the room. Everyone knew but her. "You spose to be my friend! So I know you not tellin' me you slept with the one man I'd kill ova. Are you bitch?!"

"It only happened one time!"

"I don't want to hear that shit, Brina!" she yelled jumping up and down. "You a fuckin' snake! I smelled your ass a long time ago, but I put that shit out of my mind. Thinkin' you would never betray me!" she continued approaching the bed.

"I'm sorry." Sabrina responded her hands extended out in front of her.

"Fuck that! You can't believe how much you just hurt me! I don't even have his baby and he was my man! I'm sposed to have somethin' to remember him by not you!"

Yvonna had the strong urge to hit her, but the tubes in Sabrina's arms were making her feel some kind of way. *Fuck them tubes!* She thought to herself as she smacked the fuck out of her lips.

"I deserve that." If she would've said anything else, she would've smacked her again.

"I know you did you, fishy-pussy-smellin', bitch! I know you deserve that shit! And when it happen, Brina? Huh? When you tellin' me you fucked my man?"

Sabrina was slow with her words and knew she had to choose them carefully.

"It was when ya'll weren't together no more."

"Not togetha no more? When the fuck me and Bilal ain't been togetha?"

"It was after Iesha told you she messed with him."

"You mean you fucked him 10 months ago right after I found out he was cheatin' on me with someone else?!"

She nodded yes.

"You mean you went behind my back when you knew what I

was goin' through? You lower than a snake, you ain't shit! I trusted you, Brina! Shit!" She said stomping on the hospital floor again.

"He wanted me to have the baby." Sabrina cried. "I wanted to have a abortion and he told me not to. You know how Bilal was."

The thought of Bilal wanting her to keep his baby had her on edge. She felt like blowing the entire hospital up but her sister was in it.

"Shit! Shit! Shit! I can't believe this!!!" Yvonna screamed.

Everything started spinning around in Yvonna's head. She recalled asking her to spy on Bilal when they broke up months ago. Although she was beefin' with him, she wanted to see if he really missed her, or was out fucking some other bitches. So she asked Sabrina to spy on him. Yvonna remembered the night Sabrina came back *late* with an update. And when she asked what took her so long, she claimed to have stopped by a fast food restaurant before reaching Yvonna's. She was so greedy she didn't question her.

"Girl, he ain't doin' nothing." Sabrina reported. "He love you and ya'll need to get back together."

Little did Yvonna know that instead of Sabrina scoping the scene on the outside, she had a far better view on the inside of the house he shared with his mother in Capital Heights Maryland. The sneaky bitch heard from Yvonna that Bilal had a big dick, and wanted some of it for herself. So she knocked on his door with a bag of weed, already knowing his weakness, a good high.

He was so happy to see somebody Yvonna knew because he'd missed her so much, that he didn't waste time opening the door. Besides, Sabrina told him she wanted to talk to him about Yvonna and their relationship. She claimed to be over there for Yvonna's sake and that Yvonna was miserable without him.

It was because of Sabrina that he knew where to find Yvonna and Lucy the night he approached them at Jasper's. Together they smoked the weed she got from this Jamaican cat who sold nothing but the "Truth". After the first pull, he didn't see funky pussy smelling Sabrina anymore, he saw Lela Rochan, and trust, he had to smoke a lot to get to that point.

Next thing you know she was sucking his dick and licking his ass. She tasted his entire body before she even felt his dick. By the time he fucked her, she only got to enjoy him for five minutes. And that's all it took for him to get her pregnant. He felt like shit the next day like most men do after fucking their girl's best friend. But Sabrina put him at ease by promising to never tell Yvonna about their freak fest. He trusted her considering they both knew how Yvonna was if provoked.

The first person she told she was pregnant was Bernice. Bernice wanted to stay out of it so that Bilal could handle his own affairs. Instead of going to Bilal, Sabrina told Cream. Cream cried for twenty minutes before Sabrina was able to threaten her into secrecy. All she cared about was not wanting Yvonna hurt, but Sabrina wasn't trying to hear that shit.

When Sabrina finally got the courage to tell Bilal over the phone, he told her to be outside in thirty minutes. Twenty eight minutes later, he pulled up in the front of her house in his Gold 2000 Acura 3.2 TL, and told her to get inside. He was quiet the entire time, only opening his mouth to tell her to buckle her seat belt.

When they finally stopped, they were in front of an abortion clinic. Without saying a word he dropped three hundred dollars in her lap and told her to keep the change. She got out of the car, knowing better than to fuck with Bilal. She went in pretending to be in the clinic for four hours. When she walked outside, she was shocked to see Bilal still there.

"You aight?" he asked.

"Yes," she responded.

"You know we can't tell her 'bout dis right?"

She nodded yes.

"I got your word?"

"Yes, Bilal."

"Aight…cuz what we did was a one time thing. It ain't neva happenin' again." Later he dropped her off at home hoping to sweep their little secret under the rug. But the secret got out, and it killed Yvonna.

And now in the hospital, Yvonna was thinking about the many times she ran out and got food late at night for Sabrina's pregnancy. She decided she needed to fuck her ass up again. But before she could get in another blow, Mrs. Santana entered the room and asked if everything was okay. She was talking to Sabrina and that angered Yvonna even more.

"Everything fine," she said wiping her tears. "She was just leaving." Yvonna liked how she tried to get bold all of a sudden.

"You're gonna remember this shit, Sabrina." she advised. "Before I die, I'm gonna wipe my ass with your tears."

"Maybe you should leave, Yvonna." Mrs. Santana responded.

"Let me ask you somethin'," Yvonna said desperately trying to be strong. The thought of them seeing her down fucked with her. "How long did you know she was carrying Bilal's baby?"

"I've known for months." Bernice responded without remorse. "What difference does it make?"

"You ain't nothin' but a raggedy old bitch!"

"Get out!" Mrs. Santana yelled.

"You said I was like your daughter! I thought you loved me!"

"You were like a daughter to me." she responded mustering up some fake ass tears. "But this is my grandbaby. He's like a gift to me since your father took away Bilal."

"No wonder you were so cool at the funeral. You already tryin' to replace him. I can't believe all of ya'll were laughing behind my back." she continued looking around at Cream, Sabrina and Dave who was standing in the doorway. "You gonna pay for this shit I promise you." With that she hock spit in Mrs. Santana's face.

"Yvonna! Get the fuck out of here!" Mrs. Santana replied wiping the clumpy spit from her eyes.

Cream felt like shit for her part in everything and ran behind Yvonna.

"Bitch, go back in there!" She heard her footsteps closely behind her. "You stabbed me in the back too!"

"I just found out." She lied.

"I don't give a fuck!" she yelled. "You were sposed to be my friend! You don't hold back no shit like that from me! I shoulda known a bitch who would steal somebody's husband couldn't be trusted!"

"Yvonna, don't do this to me," she cried. "I would've never participated in any of this if Sabrina didn't beg me not to say nothin' to you. I love you. You know that."

"If you loved me you would've been real with me. I'm outta here!"

Yvonna left her ass standing and crying in the hallway, but she quickly realized that there was nowhere left to run.

Chapter Six

Spiral Of Bad Luck

People whisked to and from their cars as the feeling of urgency ran through the air.

"You got a light?" Yvonna asked a stranger as she stood outside of the hospital with a Kool's Menthol cigarette in her mouth. Lately she was so disturbed that she'd adopted her old habit back.

"Naw." The stranger patted his pockets. "I was gonna ask you."

"Here you go." Crazy Dave appeared from nowhere.

Yvonna turned around and frowned at Dave who was standing beside her with a lit cigarette.

"What the fuck you want?" she asked after bending down to light her cigarette from his. When it was completely lit, she blew a puff of smoke in his face.

"I wanted to make sure you were 'aight." He paused and took another pull. "You jetted out of there like you was 'bout to pass out or somethin'."

"Yeah well I'm fine," she said with attitude as she took two steps away from him, her back turned toward him. She was mad at the world, and since she hated him anyway, she hated him even more now. "You can go back and tell them mothafuckas that I'm not trippin' off of none of this shit. That baby can rot in hell with its father for all I give a good got damn. All I need in this world is my baby sis."

"You know B only fucked that girl once right?" He continued before mashing his cigarette into the ground after only four pulls. "Why you lettin' that shit fuck wit you?"

"Dave, please!" she said stepping further away from him. "I got a lot on my mind right now and all I want to do is be left alone."

"I see why he stepped out on your ass." he frowned like he wanted to smack the shit out of her. He hated girls with fast mouths. "You a bitch!"

"Why I gotta be a bitch because I want to be left alone?"

"You a bitch because you mad at the world for no reason."

"How you sound Dave? My dead boyfriend had a baby by my best friend! And everybody was in on it!" She looked at him trying not to take note of how attractive he was.

"You need to calm down and lower your voice."

"I'm not lowerin' shit! How the fuck am I 'spose to act?"

Taking a deep breath he said, "You got a right to be heated. But errybody got problems."

"I'm not talkin' bout where I'm gonna get my next weed from problems Dave. I got *serious* problems."

"No what you *really* have is a mothafuckin' attitude. I'm tryin' to talk to you and you blowing me off."

"You wouldn't understand me anyway."

"Listen, I told him not to marry you until he told you about lil youngin'. But he told me he was gonna ask you anyway before Sabrina had the baby. He had a feelin' she was gonna tell you bout the kid cuz she kept sayin' she wanted to be with him, and he was blowin' her off."

"She wanted him to leave me?!"

"Yes." He placed his hand on her arm. "I'm just tellin' you cuz you need to know that nigga loved you. He ain't have to ask you to marry him. Most dudes would've run away from all this shit. He wanted to make things right."

"He didn't love me." She sighed.

He shook his head and said, "Whateva. That nigga loved your dirty drawers. He was just hopin' if he married you, you wouldn't leave him once you found out about his seed."

"What?" she asked looking at him sideways. "You mean he actually thought I wouldn't divorce his ass after findin' out he got

my friend pregnant? Damn," she giggled glancing at the engagement ring she was still wearing. "Bilal didn't know me after all."
She placed the ring in her pocket.

"Let me take you for a ride." He felt he laid too much on her
and she needed some fresh air.

"I'm not goin' nowhere wit you, boy."

"Come on man," he said walking closer to her. "It ain't like
you got nowhere else to go."

"Dave, maybe you don't realize it, but I don't fuck wit you. I
neva have and I neva will! So would you please leave me the fuck
alone for the umpth-mothafuckin-teenth time!"

Dave was tired of wasting his breath on her. Like he had many
times before, he flipped. No longer was he *asking*, he was now
telling her what she was going to do. He pulled her by the arm to
his black Impala that was parked in the emergency drop off parking lot, outside of the hospital. People looked at him but no one
dared stop him or get in his way.

"What is wrong wit you?" She fought hitting his muscular
arms. Her punches appeared to bounce off.

"You were my man's girl and I'm lookin' out for you!" He
opened the passenger side door, threw her inside and slammed it
shut. Afterward he jogged to the driver's side and got in.

"Are you kidnapping me, Dave?"

"Nope. I'm gettin' you some fresh air."

Her procrastination on attempting to get out of the car assured
him that she needed a break from the hospital more than she realized.

"What do you want from me?" They pulled out of the parking
lot.

"I just want you to know I understand why you beefin'."

"So what's your point?" she asked looking at the tail lights blur
as they passed them in the night.

"My point is you can take whateva you feelin' out on me." He
smiled. "I can handle it."

Silence.

If this mothafucka thinks he's getting' some pussy he can forget it.

"I can't believe you're actually smilin'," she looked at him briefly before looking away. "That's a first."

"I smile sometimes," he said trying to wipe it off. "I mean I'm not no goofy ass nigga eitha. But I do smile. I guess I neva had a reason to when you were around."

"That's cold." She giggled. And then she thought about what he said. "Please don't tell me I'm your reason. Cuz it's a little too early to be hittin' on your boy's girl."

"Naw…," he laughed. "You ain't even my type."

"I'm not your type?" She said pointing at herself. "Boy I'm every man's type."

"Damn you conceited!"

"It's true." She laughed. "I just wished I was Bilal's *only* type." Silence.

"So anyway," she continued. "What kind of girls *do* you like?"

"I like women who know what they want." he advised leaning back into his seat while steering the car with his right hand. "And you seem like you're all ova the place."

She was offended.

"I'm not all over the place!"

"You sure?" he asked sarcastically raising his right eyebrow. "I heard rumors about you. People say yo ass is crazy."

"Listen," she said looking at him with squinted eyes. "Don't ever call me that shit again! I hate when people call me crazy."

"Yeah aight," he said as if he wasn't paying her any mind.

"I'm serious!"

"And I said aight!" he continued with enough base in his voice to remind her that he was a thug who couldn't be bossed around. "What your ass need is a vacation," he said nodding his head. "And quick too." he grabbed a bag of weed and a pack of cherry Philly Blunts from his glove compartment and threw them in her lap. "You know how to roll?"

She was angry at his disrespect. She was born in the hood and learning how to roll a blunt was a requirement.

You playin' right?"

He chuckled.

"Wait a minute." She said cracking the blunt and emptying its contents to repack it with the weed. "How you callin' me crazy when you go by Crazy Dave?"

"I'm just giving my perspective."

"And when did you become Dr. Phil?"

"When you got in my car."

"You mean when you kidnapped me. Anyway, I know what I want and I know who I am, and crazy is the furthest thing from me."

"That's what you say." He responded watching the precision she used with rolling the blunt. After it was tightly wound, she licked it shut. She was being extra sexy with running her wet tongue up and down the sides and Dave was turned on. "Where your lighter?"

He handed it to her and she ran the heat along the sides until it hardened.

"You're the one who gets all fucked up when you don't get your way," she continued firing it up. "You gonna be a thug all your life." She blew out smoke and passed it to him.

"I got shit I want to do." He said accepting the handoff.

"Like what? I gotta hear this shit."

"I want to work wit kids and stuff?"

She burst out into laughter.

"What?" He was confused by her laughter.

"I can't see you workin' wit *kids* and *stuff*."

"Why not?"

"For one you're gettin' high while driving," she laughed. "Second you's a hot head."

"That's what you think?"

"Yeah." she nodded. "That's what I know. Ain't *that's* why they call you Crazy Dave?"

"No...," he responded turning onto Alabama Avenue on the south side of D.C. "They call me Crazy because people say I'm impulsive or some shit like that. But I don't think that's the case. I think-,"

EEEEERRRRRRR...BOOOOOOOMMMMMM.....

Out of nowhere a semi truck came from the left and pummeled the Impala. Dave's neck snapped to the back before his head hit the dashboard. Yvonna's body flew to the front before being tossed around inside like a rag doll. The car rolled over six times before finally landing on the back wheels and then the front. It was completely demolished. And just when things were already worse, two other cars ran smack into them, and Dave was instantly thrown through the windshield ending up on the passenger side face down on the ground. Yvonna on the other hand lay unconscious in what use to be the back seat. This would spawn the wrath of her anger.

Chapter Seven

Sick And Tired

A *n irritated and cranky* baby cried out loud, "Are you okay?" Sabrina asked.

"What are you doin' here?" Yvonna said sitting up in the hospital bed. She wiped her eyes and noticed every muscle in her body ached.

"We came to make sure you were okay. We still care about you even though you mad at us." Sabrina said parading the baby around in front of her.

"Well I don't want ya'll here." She said as she looked at Cream who was also in the room.

"Yvonna, please," Cream responded already on the verge of crying. She hated when she was mad at her. "Don't treat us like this. We're still your friends. You bein' mad at us won't bring Bilal back."

"Bitch, what are you talking about?" Yvonna said in a condescending tone. "You ain't my fuckin' friend!"

"Yes I am." She wiped her tears. "We both are."

"You called?" the nurse asked entering the room. She came on queue because Yvonna activated the assistance needed button without notice. She was a short stout woman with extremely dark skin. Her white nurse shoes leaned outwardly due to how she walked. Her arms were extremely hairy and the name on her badge said Penny. "Is everything awight wit cha?" she reached out to check her IV and her knuckles were dark.

"No," she paused as she watched the woman fuss over her. "I want them bitches out of here!"

As if she was an energizer bunny who was turned the other way she immediately focused on the outsiders. "You heard her!" she said grabbing Cream first since she was the closest to the door. "Ya'll have to leave! We can't have people disturbin' the patients. Specially none of the ones who's in my care." She seemed more than willing to carry out functions fitting of a bodyguard.

Before they could get two words out edgewise, they were being thrown out on their asses.

"I'm sorry, sweetie," Penny said after the room was cleared. "I didn't know theys were in here botherin' you. They practically been here ever since they brought you in. We just happy you conchus now."

"Thank you," she said feeling as if the pain was suddenly getting worse. "But just so you know, I ain't got no friends or family so I don't want nobody in here."

"Say no more," she said checking her blood pressure and vitals. "I'm a loana too!"

Yvonna produced a half of smile. "Do you have anything to give me for this pain?"

"The docta will be in her shortly. You can ask her," She continued as she diligently filled out the chart next to her bed. "I'ma go get her now."

When she left, Yvonna finally had a chance to look around the room. Everything was so drab and depressing. Right down to the old yellow comforter on the bed. The only life in the room was the three flower vases across from her. Out of all of them, one stood out more. The name Dave was written in black magic marker on the outside of the tiny white envelope. Yvonna was just about to go read it until the doctor entered the room.

"Don't get up. You have stitches in places you wouldn't imagine." Yvonna sat back down.

She was 5'9 and looked more like a model than a doctor. Her coal black hair was swept into an elaborate bun and she looked neat and crisp. She favored Angelina Jolie more than a little bit.

"How you doing, sweetheart?" Her voice was kind and warm. She sounded so sincere, Yvonna almost started crying. It was the first time since everything happened that someone appeared to have a genuine concern for her.

"Not so good." She said holding her head.

"I can imagine. But I'm happy you're alive. You should've seen the pictures of the car." she softly touched her shoulder.

"I guess I should be grateful huh?"

"Yes, you should."

"Do you know anything about the guy who was with me?"

"Yes. He's fine! He's been up here five or six times already. Outside of walking with a cane for the next few months I'd say he's blessed too."

Part of her was happy he was concerned about her, but the other part hated that this was his fault. Had he not taken her against her will, this would've never happened. And had Sabrina not slept with her man, she would've never been upset.

"How long have I been here?"

"Two whole weeks."

"Oh my God!"

"I know," she giggled. "It seemed like it was just yesterday. Would you believe that Penny predicted you'd come around today. She's been fussing over you ever since you got here. She says God told her you needed *extra* care."

Yvonna was so concerned with *who did what and when*, that she didn't catch the message.

"Can I have somethin' for this pain?"

"Sure," she said digging in her pocket to get the syringe filled with Morphine. "I was going to ask if you felt you needed this or not. But I never like to suggest pain meds unless a patient requests." She walked over to the IV and inserted the morphine directly into the tube. "Better yet?"

She nodded yes as the medicine began to take hold of her body.

"I have to tell you something, Ms. Harris."

"What is it?" She questioned hoping it wasn't about her sister. "Is my sister okay?"

"Yes she's fine. They left a message for you earlier. It's about your pregnancy. We weren't able to save the baby."

"Huh…I don't understand. I didn't have a baby."

"But you did Ms. Harris," her response was in a careful and sensitive tone. "I'm sorry."

The room began to spin and Yvonna was no longer able to hear the doctor's voice. She missed hearing that the car accident was so bad, that part of the dashboard entered her abdomen giving her an instant abortion.

All Yvonna thought about was the lost of something she never knew she had, a baby. She thought the morning sickness she was experiencing the past couple of weeks was *just* something that came over her.

"Ms. Harris! Ms. Harris! Are you alright?"

Yvonna was so distraught that she was drifting out of consciousness again. And when she came to, she'd be a different person, filled with hate and motives for revenge. The old Yvonna Harris died with the news of the lost of her baby, and the new Yvonna would be someone who would forever hold a grudge.

Chapter Eight

Pop, Pop Fizz
6 Months Later

*H*is *heavy breathing* irritated the hell out of Yvonna. Theodorus's stomach rose and fell with every breath he made. His dick was unusually large considering he was certifiably obese.

This is what her life consisted of now, whoring. She had nothing else to live for. The only person she loved she left behind. The first day she arrived in Baltimore she called Jhane' to ask her to say goodbye to Jesse for her. Losing her baby hurt and she knew she had to leave. So she took two hundred and sixty seven dollars and jumped on a train. And now here she was penniless and alone.

"You gonna do it or not?" he asked staring at Yvonna who was standing at the foot of the bed, threatening not do what she agreed.

Fat ass dog! She thought as she eyeballed him, trying to determine if she should reduce herself to what he wanted done.

But when she looked at the table next to the motel bed, and realized she had seven dollars and eighty nine cents to her name, she knew exactly what needed to be done. She didn't have tricks calling her anymore like they use to, because word got around that she was the whore with too many standards.

She'd tell them quick, *I'm not doin' this and I'm not doing that.* A lot of times they'd leave not completely satisfied. So when Theodorus, the fat janitor who maintained the motel rooms called her today, she jumped at the chance to make some extra cash.

Before he even stepped foot in her room, he made it clear what he wanted done. His fetish consisted of pleasure mixed with pain.

And out of all the nasty shit she had to do in her life, his preference was the worse. Because his dusty ass got off when women burst the pimples on his back, and with their tongue, licked the puss.

"Stop wastin' my fuckin' time!" he yelled as the whites of his eyes shown through the dark room. "What you waitin' on?!"

"Give me a second damn!" She thought about being put out on the street if she didn't give the money for rent to the owner of the run down motel in Baltimore city she stayed in by tomorrow. "Turn over."

Without hesitating, he rotated himself almost breaking the bed frame underneath him. Judging by his breathing, she could tell rolling around was a chore.

"Ouch!" he hollered bouncing his huge head off of the edge of the wooden dresser, next to the bed. "Come on!" he yelled not giving her a chance to make her way over to him on her own. "Why you standin' there lookin' like a statue, you could be ova here finishin' me off."

The idea of being done with it gave her enough energy to get started. She slowly crawled on top of him. Her bare vagina was directly touching his back. He liked it that way. She flipped the lamp on to get a good look at the bumps he had on his skin. When she did, she was disgusted at the sight before her eyes. He had ten or eleven huge puss bumps all over him. She thought it was convenient that a man who liked his bumps burst as a means to get off, would have so many of them.

"How did you get all of these on your back?!" she asked as a wave of nausea passed.

"Why you wanna know? Just do it!"

"Just askin'." She said eyeing the smallest one first.

"I get em from my sweaty work shirts." He informed, excited at the chance of finally getting his rocks off. His hormones were raging and she could tell he wanted her to hurry up. "I can't be wet for too long or I'll get bumps on my back. Now are you finished askin' questions?!"

She didn't answer. She just zeroed in on the bump and popped it until the puss oozed out.

"Mmmmmmm," he moaned loving the stinging pain. "Now lick it!!"

Bending down slowly trying to prevent the apple she had earlier from coming back up, she closed her eyes, and licked the outside of the bump instead of its contents.

"Stop playin' wit me, bitch!" he yelled raising his head to look at her. "I said lick the fuckin' bump!"

How the fuck he know I didn't?.

"Aight!" She contemplated putting him out, but didn't.

She bent down, extended her tongue and licked the salty remnants from his back. It tasted like a raw onion in her mouth.

"That's right, beautiful," He moaned. "Do another one."

Again she popped a bump and licked the puss from it. Her stomach churned and she begged him not to make her do it again.

"Come on!" He yelled. "Just two more and you're done." He struggled to reach underneath his huge body and between his legs to grab his dick to jerk off. She tilted a little to the side since she was on his back.

"Give me my money first. And then I'll do another."

"You don't trust me?" he asked looking back at her again.

"Naw," she said remembering the last time she trusted anybody and how it ended. "I trust no one."

Lifting his head, he reached for his wallet with the same hand he used to beat his dick. After that, he pulled out 6 twenty dollar bills throwing them on the table.

"You happy now?" he asked as he reached for his dick again. "Now finish! I gotta go home to my wife!"

Yvonna allowed him to use her mouth as a dirty cloth. She could feel him tugging at his self and for a second, she thought he'd rip the mothafucka off. When he screamed out in ecstasy, she couldn't wait to brush her teeth after throwing up in the toilet.

When he left, she crawled up in a ball on the bed, and took an "E" pill she saved for the moments she was at her lowest. If ever there was a time, now was it. She downed some of the warm coke she had in a can on the table to wash the pill down.

The can was there so long, that it completely lost its fizz. Placing the can back down she noticed the newspaper which sat under it. It read, *"Office Assistant Needed For A Growing Business. No experience necessary"*.

She jumped out of bed thinking the ring was a sign. With the taste of the janitor still in her mouth, she called the number in the paper hoping it would be a chance at a new life.

Chapter Nine

Before I Go

She couldn't believe it. One day she was getting off the bus after an interview and the next minute she was looking at Gabriella, her long lost friend. She hadn't seen her in a long time. She looked just like Taraji Henson from the movie *Baby Boy*. Yvonna couldn't believe she was living in Baltimore all this time. All that mattered was that she was back in her life.

"Why you gonna give up easy money to work a nine to five?!" Gabriella asked Yvonna as she polished her toes on the edge of Yvonna's motel room bed.

92.Q was playing *Girls, Girls, Girls* by Jay-Z on the radio. And the cramped room had the smell of incense burning throughout it. The blunt Yvonna was smoking relaxed her.

"Cuz I'm tired of doin' nasty shit like suckin' mothafucka's bumps," she responded as she plopped on the bed causing Gabriella to polish her toe instead of her nail. "That was the grosses shit I've ever experienced in life!"

"Damn you fat bitch! Look what you did!"

"Sorry! You got to work on your steady hand!" she laughed.

"Ain't nothin' wrong with these." Gabriella wiggled them. "And at least I'm not goin' to waste em on no borin' ass job. You made one hundred and twenty dollars in fifteen minutes fuckin' wit Theodorus. It's gonna take you a day and a half *maybe* more to make it at the doctors office."

"I'd rather work a real job."

"Don't let him get into your head and shit," Gabriella advised.

"Doctors always trying to make somebody think they crazy."

"I'm not. But I can't do this shit no more. You shoulda seen Theodorus's back! Yuck!"

"I ain't gonna lie that was some nasty ass shit. You know what we should do before you leave this fucked up motel right?"

"What?"

"Pay his ass back." She said looking into her eyes.

Gabriella was everything Yvonna wanted to be. She was bold, confrontational and most of all beautiful. She did what she wanted without regard for what people thought about her. She smoked as much weed as she wanted and popped as many pills as she felt necessary to feel good. She was ruthless and sometimes uncompromising.

"I really don't know about this, Gabriella. Every time I do something you want me to, I get myself into trouble."

"That's not true."

"Yes it is." Yvonna advised. "When the smoke clears, I'm the only one standin'."

"I'm not goin' to leave your side anymore. I promise," Gabriella replied hugging her. "But we gotta get him back. And if we get caught, I'll take the wrap."

Silence

"Payback how?" Yvonna inquired.

"I got an idea that will make you feel better about what he made you do." Gabriella replied. "Let's give him a taste of his own medicine."

"Well…," Yvonna said growing tired of the lead on. "Are you gonna tell me or what?"

"The question is not if I'm gonna tell you," she responded smacking her lips. "The question is if you'll be willing to carry things out."

Without saying anything more, Yvonna already knew whatever Gabriella wanted her to do would be final.

~~~~~~

Theodorus walked up to the motel room door wearing his

brown uniform. He was breathing heavily as usual, his face drenched with sweat. He wiped his head with the dirty white hand towel he didn't leave his house without.

"You gonna let me in or not?" he asked as he waited outside of the room, eyeing Yvonna as if he wanted to fuck her right there.

"Of course," she grinned swinging the door wide open. "Come in."

Yvonna knew she looked edible tonight. It was her last night in that run down ass motel in Baltimore, and she'd managed to find a room for rent not too far from her new job.

"I hope you not tryin' to make me leave my wife," he said as he sat in the chair at the table. "Cuz I ain't leavin' my wife for no whore."

Yvonna felt like smacking the shit out of him. Trying to take him away from his crack head ass wife was not even a thought.

"Don't worry daddy," she smiled. "After I'm done, you'll be begging to go back home to her."

"What the fuck is that supposed to mean?"

"Nothing," she winked. "Just kidding'"

"Yeah whateva." he said waving her off. To be a hot ass mess, he had the arrogance fitting of a king. "So what's the occasion? You miss big daddy or somethin'?"

"Of course," she lied as she watched him try to sit comfortably at the small table in the motel room. His stomach was in the way, forcing him to hold his breath to prevent from knocking it over. Yvonna pulled the table a little from his body so he'd have room. He didn't bother thanking her.

"So where's the food!" he asked licking his black cracked lips. "You said we were having dinner first so I didn't bother eaten' before I got here."

"It's right here." She removed two white Styrofoam containers from the brown paper bag before sitting them on the table.

"Yeah," he said rubbing his belly. "And when I'm done with this, I'll fuck the shit out of that pretty wet pussy. And then I'll let you suck my dick. I know how much you like that."

He glanced down at her feet and licked his lips after seeing the red polish on her toes. The color turned him on even if it was done sloppily.

"What the fuck is that smell?" He grumbled after smelling a foul odor.

"It's your dinner honey," she responded slyly.

When he flipped open the container, he saw two large brown objects inside. He jumped up from the table, knocking everything to the floor. The shit chunks rolled out in front of him and he was disgusted.

"What the fuck is wrong wit you, you crazy bitch?!"

"What did you call me?" she snapped.

"I called you a crazy bitch!" he responded not picking up on the way her voice had changed.

"Don't talk to him no more!" Gabriella responded exiting from the bathroom. "Just do what we planned."

"What the fuck is going on around here? Have you lost your mind or something?!"

"Do it!" Gabriella yelled, growing irritated at his arrogance and lack of fear.

When he bent down to pick up his sweaty towel, Yvonna took the bat she had next to the bed, and knocked him in his head. She didn't realize how hard she hit him.

His large body fell on the floor causing the entire motel room to shake. He held on to the wound she caused and his face was inches away from the shit.

"I bet you don't have too much to say now," Yvonna responded taunting him. "Now pick up the shit, put it in your mouth, and swallow it."

"I'm not puttin' that in my mouth!" He tried to get up while holding his head. And when he went to lunge at her, he noticed his equilibrium was fucked up and wobbled toward the floor.

"Hit his ass again!" Gabriella screamed. "And if he opens his mouth this time don't stop hittin' him until he shuts the fuck up."

Without saying another word and on Gabriella's command, she hit him two more times. One of the blows landed on the previous wound causing it to bust open wider.

"Please stop hitting me!" He cried. "What did I ever do to you?"

"Oh you don't remember?" Yvonna said in a psychotic tone. "Isn't that something cuz I can't seem to forget."

"Please, Yvonna…," he cried out. "Don't do this."

He didn't sound like the manly old fart he was when he was passing out orders. He was now humble and begging for his life.

"Fuck you! Now pick it up and eat it!" she responded looking at his blood all over the floor and on her legs.

He looked up at her with half of his eye hanging out. Sobbing like a baby, he placed the broken shit in his mouth.

"Now swallow!" she demanded watching him chew her shit.

He did. She could tell he wanted to gag and she warned him about what would happen if he did. He appeared to be falling in and out of consciousness as he completed the gross task.

"You know we gonna have to finish him off right?" Gabriella asked watching him. "If you leave him alive, he'll say somethin'."

"Do we have to, Gabriella?"

"What do you think? Do you honestly think he won't say somethin'? You know what we have to do, Yvonna!"

"I don't think I can," Yvonna responded as the bat dropped down making a clinking sound on the floor. "He won't say anything."

"Fuck it! Just like always, I have to bail you out." Gabriella picked up the bat. In her bare feet wearing blue jean shorts, and a white shirt, she beat him until all the life was drained from his body.

Yvonna was scared and never thought she'd be a part of his murder. She only agreed to make him feel as fucked up as he made her feel.

After the bloody bath scene, Yvonna and Gabriella wiped the entire motel room clean of all their fingerprints. Luckily for Yvonna she changed rooms earlier because Theodorus felt the one she stayed in before, was too close to the office. And his wife, who also worked at the motel cleaning rooms, might've seen them. Because of that, there was no trace of Yvonna renting the room anywhere on record and nobody saw her go in.

Tomorrow morning, when his wife Cara came to clean up, she'd find her dead husband sprawled out on the motel floor. And Yvonna would be long gone.

Chapter Ten

4 Years Later
Can't Forgive, Can't Forget

Maxwell, Raheem Davaughn and Anthony Hamilton played on rotation in the upscale Baltimore city row home. The lights were dim and provided a sexy atmosphere to an already luxurious house. Plush white carpet covered the floors and the furniture was shipped over from Greece. In the kitchen the smell of salmon covered in a caramel candy coating, garlic mash potatoes and fresh broccoli was abundant.

Twenty-two year old Yvonna pranced around her eight thousand dollar kitchen awaiting the arrival of her prominent fiancé who was also a distinguished psychiatrist. As she had many times before, she prepared the dinner in nothing but a thong, her clothes folded neatly on the mahogany chair in the dining room.

You stung, as if you'd knew I sting right there. And you should-n't know these things, about me. Abused, as if your pain would quench my fear. How could you know these things, about me? Yvonna sang along with Maxwell's song "Know These Things".

"There she goes," Terrell Shines said walking into their home. "The one woman that makes my day every day." Placing his briefcase by the door, he walked over to the kitchen toward Yvonna. Wrapping his arms around her waist, he kissed her softly on the neck. The smell of the Light Blue cologne he wore by Dolce & Gabbana was intoxicating.

"Hey you." She smiled.

No matter how many times he saw Yvonna, he couldn't get over how attractive she was. After the breast enhancement and tummy tuck he spent thousands on, she was as close to perfection as you could get.

"You're making my favorite meal I see. What's the occasion?" He questioned rubbing her flat tummy. Looking over her shoulder at the meal simmering on the stove, he marveled at how multi-talented she was. Yvonna traded her long hair for a short style which only needed mousse to work for her. The coal black color along with the smoky eye shadow she wore regularly gave her an alluring and mysterious appeal.

"I have a surprise for you," she responded before handing him a glass of Merlot in a real crystal glass. "And I want you to always remember tonight."

Yvonna had become well rounded in the four years since she'd left DC. Being a doctor's fiancé came at a price. She had to stop speaking slang and handle herself like a lady, always.

"Wow," he said walking over to the table to sift through the mail. "Usually I'm the one surprising you."

Terrell was white and black mixed with somewhat bronze colored skin due to having Indian within his family. He stood 6'4 and was definitely noticed when he walked into a room. Everyone wondered how a girl who before was only his secretary, eventually got him to propose, and they didn't bother asking knowing she would never reveal her secrets. She was a loaner, allowing only three people near her.

"I know honey," she responded placing a plate in front of him. "But the tables are turning tonight."

"Well this should be interesting."

"It will," she winked sitting on the other side of the table across from him. Her bare breasts bouncing around gave Terrell and immediate hard on. She sat her plate in front of her and nibbled on the salmon she prepared.

"So how was your day honey?" She questioned sipping some of the wine in her glass. "I trust you had a good one."

"It was okay. We had a patient return today. Apparently he had a serious reaction from the meds I prescribed him. So he came in cursing out my staff and they eventually had to escort him out."

"A serious reaction?" she repeated. "How?"

"It seems his allergies were overlooked when I went over his chart. I tried to apologize for the mishap but he wasn't buying it. And now he's threatening to sue me."

"What?!"

"Yeah it was awful." He gobbled what was left of the salmon before moving over to the broccoli. "But my lawyers will eat him alive. He hasn't the slightest idea who he's dealing with."

"But I do!" Yvonna responded licking her full sexy lips. "Is there anything I can do?"

"Actually the moment I saw you, my day became better." He wiped his mouth with the cloth napkin on his lap.

For a second Yvonna looked at Terrell. Rich was an understatement when referring to him. His ten thousand dollar Rolex alone made it clear what his bank account looked like. And if there was any more doubt, the red custom made corvette in their double garage could vouch for his status.

After they talked some more about their days, she walked over to the end of the table and straddled him. She playfully unbuttoned his slacks and allowed his stiff dick to come out to play. Kissing him softly on the lips she inserted him into her warm, wet pussy.

"Mmmmmmmm," he moaned as he suckled her bottom lip. "How come I can never get enough of you?"

"Because I'm a handful," she smiled.

He placed his hands on both sides of her waist and pumped in and out of her until he felt himself preparing to release.

"Can I stay?" he was referring to staying inside of her when he bust. In the past she told him to pull out because she hated how his cum always stayed in her body for days after they had sex. It made her feel nasty. But today, she'd make and exception.

"Yes baby," she said placing her lips over top of his. "You can –,"

Before she could finish her statement he'd already released himself inside of her body. He was trembling and for a minute she thought he was having a seizure, but then she remembered…her pussy was that good.

"Outstanding." he complimented. She kissed his lips and slid her tongue inside his mouth. "Did you cum?" She hated when he asked her that because she never did.

"No, baby," she smiled kissing him again. "I didn't."

"I'll last longer next time."

"It's okay, honey."

In the bedroom he was a mess and he made promises he couldn't keep. His fuck game was trash and that was the only problem she had with him. *Well*…that and the fact that he was weaker than she liked her men to be.

"I just wish I could satisfy you more." he whined. "I want to be everything to you Yvonna." He rubbed his hands on her back stroking up and down.

"You've given me everything I've ever wanted. I never required anything more from you." she replied softly. "I'm happy for that."

"So what's your surprise?" he asked bringing himself to another hard on. "Because in a minute I'll be ready for another round."

"Oh, I almost forgot. Well, honey…I'm leaving you."

"What?" he chuckled.

"I said," she smiled kissing him. "I'm leaving you."

"You're playing right?" His eyes searched hers for answers.

"No I'm not, Terrell. I'm not playing at all." Sensing he finally understood, she stood up and put on her clothes. "Awww…don't look so sad baby, we had fun while it lasted."

"You mind telling me what's going on Yvonna?"

"Sure." She said as if they were discussing the weather instead of the end of their relationship. "I have everything I came for. And trust me baby, this isn't because of anything you did." She fixed her clothes. "It's just that I have some unfinished business to take care of and I can't do it here."

"I can help you," he stood up adjusting his pants. "With anything you need but please don't leave me, Yvonna."

"I'm sooooo sorry, Terrell." she said placing her purse on the table. "But I already have."

"Why are you so cold all of a sudden? Who are you?"

The question carried more weight than he realized. Since the first day she began working for him four years ago, Yvonna knew her master plan. In an effort to never get hurt again, she wrote down goals and stuck to them. Anything not in her plan she fought, including love. One of her goals was to meet someone wealthy and convince him to take care of her. And she found that in Terrell.

The only person she cared about she abandoned and that was her sister Jesse. But while working for Terrell, she saw something in his eyes when he looked at her. She knew if she kept him close, he would fall for her and she was right. From the streets or not, Yvonna was sexy and wild and that alone appealed to the good doctor.

Slowly she evolved into a woman learning everything about the games of the mind from him. In fact, it was from his very books that she learned how to fool even him into believing she was in love. Eventually 26 year old Terrell dumped his white girlfriend of ten years and moved a young black Yvonna into his home, instead. He spared no expense on her.

But there was always an ulterior motive for Yvonna. She wanted to pay back everyone who made the list of people she hated the most. Every lie she told, every breath she took was dedicated to getting revenge. Outside of Gabriella, 26 year old Caven Cooks, one of Terrell's old patients was the only one she kept close. She knocked down any other possibility for friendships for fear of being stabbed in the back again.

"Who am I?" she asked herself glancing up at the cathedral ceilings before looking back at him. "I'm somebody you should've never come in contact with. Maybe under different circumstances you and I could've been…but that time is not now."

Beep…beep….beep.

Yvonna walked over to the window and looked out. She smiled when she saw Caven's Red Denali waiting. He parked next to Yvonna's candy apple red BMW which she would be leaving.

"Well I have to go?"

"You're leaving me for, Caven?" he asked stealing a peek at who was waiting for her outside. "I thought ya'll were just friends!

You do realize he isn't well don't you? That's why he was my patient."

"I know, honey. But don't worry about us. And don't worry about my things or my car because I have everything I need, including eighty thousand dollars in cash you gave me access to."

"What?" he said grabbing her arm.

"Unless you wanna die" her voice was calm and terrifying. "I suggest you take your fucking hands off of me."

He slowly and reluctantly complied.

"You're not going to get away with this Yvonna."

"I already did."

With that she dropped her keys on the floor and walked out the door.

Chapter Eleven

The Games Began

The sound of the engine humming and beeping from the busy roads irritated Yvonna.

"You okay?" Asked Caven. His natural hazel eyes looked upon her with admiration and appreciation.

"I'm fine, honey," she smiled. "Thanks for being on time."

She clicked her seat belt and pulled a black leather book from her Gucci purse. The book was specially made for Yvonna and she wrote in it everyday. She read somewhere that if you wanted something to happen, you had to *will* it. The book was engraved in gold and read "*Yvonna*" on the cover.

"How'd he take it?" Caven asked merging onto the highway, stealing a look at the book he always saw her carry.

"How would you take it if I cut you out my life?" *Silence.* "He'll live." She continued.

When he looked at the book again he saw some names in dark brown on the white pages. It looked as if they were written in blood. She'd hired a private detective to tell her everything she needed to know about what they were doing in their lives. She knew where they worked, who they were with and where they lived.

"Well I'm happy we're finally taking care of this," he responded referring to the lies she told him about all the awful things people did to her. "It's about time they pay for what they did to you."

"I'm happy too." She focused again on the pen in her hands and the personalized book in her lap. "Now if you can give me a few moments of silence I'd appreciate it."

"Sure...let me know when you're ready to talk." With that he turned the music up softly.

"Honey," she said touching his hand still attached to the volume button. "I said silence." With that she turned the radio off.

Opening the cover, she glanced at the names before her. So much time had passed and finally they'd get what they deserved.

Bilal Santana
Bernice Santana
Cream Justice
Sabrina Beddows
Dave Walters

She tore the page off and tucked it in her pocket.

"Better now?" Caven asked glancing over at Yvonna who was staring at him.

Instead of answering him she said, "Pull over."

"Here?" He asked confused.

"Yes...over on the left."

He obeyed, like he always did whenever she gave him orders. When they were on the shoulder of the highway, she quickly removed her seat belt and moved toward him. When she was free, she covered his lips with hers.

"I want you to kiss it for me."

He felt her request strange but said, "Of course," as he pushed her panties to the side and ran his tongue around her clit. She didn't care that he'd be tasting Terrell's jizz. Revenge got her aroused and she wanted to be pleased.

Caven was captivated by her and Yvonna knew it. She mind fucked him so much that she actually had him thinking he couldn't live without her.

"You love me?" She questioned as she palmed the back of his head, offering him little room to speak.

"Yes," he managed. "I do."

"You'd do anything for me?"

"Yes."

"So help me get back at the people who ruined my life."

"I'll do anything you want me to," he responded as he ferociously licked her pussy.

When he said that she pulled him closer and he could barely breathe. She didn't care. Just as long as he remained in her control and did what was asked of him, he'd be safe. And if not, he'd be expendable too.

Chapter Twelve

Even After Death, Hate Lives
Bilal Santana

*T*res *rolling over the loose* rocks played in the background. "You sure you want to go alone?" Caven asked. He wondered what was so important at a graveyard that couldn't wait until morning.

"Positive. Wait here." Yvonna was preparing to rush out the door the moment the car stopped at the Fort Lincoln cemetery.

"I thought you had to go to the bathroom?" Caven questioned feeling weird about her moving along in the night.

"I do. And I'll be right back.

When the car stopped, she moved toward the huge black marble tombstone. She found out where his plot was from the caretaker last week. Bilal's picture behind the glass casing appeared to be staring her down as she stepped toward it. She looked around the grass and noticed many flowers arrangements. Four years ago today he was killed. She figured the flowers came from his mother and friends. But it was the small yellow toy car that angered her. Placing her purse on the marble bench next to the grave, she walked closer to his headstone.

"Hello, Bilal. It's been a long time. Well…for me it seems like just yesterday. Sorry I didn't come earlier, it's just that," she paused and cleared her throat. "I couldn't see you until I was ready. I don't know if it's possible for you to look at my life, but if you have, you'll see I've changed. Living in Baltimore has made me more refined. It's like I've gotten an education without even going to college."

Yvonna walked to the bench next to the tombstone and sat down. The moonlight radiated her beauty, hate and love all at the same time.

"I stopped by to tell you that you hurt me. Up until today, I've never told another soul how you made me feel except Gabriella. We were in love Bilal! I woulda, done anything for you. Why would you betray me in life and death? It wasn't enough for you to sleep with someone else, you had to sleep with one of my closest friends too. And then you gave her a baby!" She lowered her voice when she heard it echoing throughout the cemetery.

Silence.

She stood up and said, "Well...nothing matters much anymore. You're right where you belong...in hell!"

Suddenly she lifted her skirt, and allowed her panties to drop to her ankles. She placed one hand on the bench for balance, squatted and shitted on his grave. When she was done she took the engagement ring that she clutched in her hand and tossed it in the mess.

Adjusting her clothes, she grabbed a stone and cracked the casing which held his picture. It shattered into a million pieces. Then and only then did she return to the car satisfied.

"You ready?" Caven asked when she got in.

She wore a look of pleasure on her face like a new pair of shoes. Dealing with Bilal was just the beginning.

"Yes," she smiled. "I'm ready."

With that she removed the gold tip fountain pin filled with blood and crossed Bilal Santana's name off the list. One down and many more to go.

Chapter Thirteen

Different News
Bernice Santana

Water from the kitchen sink ran and was forgotten about as Bernice fussed over her grandson.

"Who is it?" She asked after just recently preparing her four year old grandson's lunch. Someone was at the door. She couldn't hear them answer so she turned off the water. "Damn it!" she yelled wiping her hand on her apron.

"They not dere grand mommy." The little boy said his legs swinging under his body on the blue chair.

"Can you be a good little boy while mommy answers the door?" She placed the neatly sliced bologna and cheese sandwich on his plate.

"You not mommy." He informed. "You grand mommy."

"I know. But you know what I mean. Can you be good for me?"

"I'll try." He sang.

She reached down and kissed his cheek with her MAC glossy lips. Years had passed and Bernice was still beautiful and fly. And after all this time, she *still* never got a job. Looking better than most forty-somethin' women her age, she managed to land a man who worked as a bus driver. He was making pretty good money and loved spending it on his Spanish mami. She almost broke him but he knew she was expensive before he started dealing with her. Louis Vuitton, was her fetish and she had lots of it courtesy of her blue collar beau.

Bernice smiled realizing how much Lil Bilal acted and looked like her son. To her it was like she was raising Bilal all over again.

"Well you betta try to be good harder this time," she responded remembering the last time she turned her back on him. Everything that belonged in the refrigerator was spread out on the kitchen floor. Lil Bilal, was a terror and it didn't help that Sabrina spoiled him rotten.

Wiping her hands on her apron again, she walked to the door and looked out the peephole.

"Who is it?" She saw a tall handsome man and wondered who he was. She also glanced at the red truck on the curb in front of her home.

"A old friend of your son's." his voice was warm and considerate.

"W…wha..aat?" she stuttered.

"I said I'm an old friend of Bilal's…please open the door. I'd like to talk to you."

Bernice turned around and leaned up against the door. Bilal had died so long ago, that the mere mentioning of his name bothered her at times. She even had problems calling her grandson Bilal Jr., and she often referred to him as "baby".

Looking around her cozy home she wondered what kind of friend he was, and why she never saw him before. Surely if he was a real friend, she would've known him.

Although she'd come to the realization that Bilal had passed, she did so without dealing with his death. She used Bilal Jr., as a vehicle to mask her pain. She hadn't even shed a tear since she buried him.

Standing up straight, she dusted herself off and pulled open the door.

"Your name?"

"I'm, Caven Boyd. May I come in?" She didn't get the vibe that he'd do her any harm. So on the strength of mentioning Bilal's name, she allowed a stranger to enter her home.

"Please come in."

Once inside he made himself comfortable on the sofa.

"Your home's beautiful," he responded crossing his legs, as he cupped his knees. His mannerisms feminine.

"Thank you," she responded as she glanced over at the kitchen to make sure Bilal Jr., was okay. "You alright, baby?"

"Yes…I'm a big boy grand mommy."

"Good, baby," She giggled at his response. "Stay good just a little while longer. We have company."

Directing her attention back to the stranger, she glanced over him. He was far neater and more reserved than the friends she'd seen Bilal hang with before he passed. His hazel eyes, light brown skin and statuesque features made him look regal.

"How can I help you, Mr. Boyd?" she questioned sitting back in her chair, her eyes glued onto his.

"I just heard." he said calmly.

"About what?"

"Bilal's death."

Her son's name and the word death sent spikes through her heart.

"Oh…," she responded clearing her throat. "My son has been dead for quite some time now."

"I know. And I don't mean to cause you any pain, but Bilal was very close to me."

"Really?"

"Yes." He reassured her. "So hearing about his death troubled me. I had to come over to see if it was true."

"It's funny," she said getting up to grab two cups of coffee. "I never heard him mention your name before. Two sugars or one?" she continued yelling from the kitchen.

"I like mine extra *sswweeeeet.*" His words drug out. "So you can bring as much sugar as you can spare."

Walking back into the living room, she placed the wooden tray of coffee on the table.

"Did you run with the YMB?"

He giggled and corrected her, "The YBM and no mam. They would've never accepted someone like me in."

"Oh? And why not?"

"Because I wasn't as thuggish as most of the members were.

I'm more reserved, and *private*. Bilal was the same way."

"You sure you're my son's friend?" She chuckled although deadly serious. "Because he was very thuggish, more than I liked him to be sometimes." She lied. She loved his thuggish qualities because the harder he appeared, the more respected he would be out in the streets. And the more respect he earned, the more money he'd make.

"I'm *sure* I was very much his friend," he continued sipping the coffee in his white porcelain cup. "And if I'm not being too presumptuous, I'd say I was his closest friend."

"Really?" she said raising her eyebrow. She recalled Dave being his closest friend. "Where are you from again? And where did you meet Bilal?"

He smiled. Placed the cup down and sat up straight.

"I met him by accident. It was almost as if we were meant to meet. Bilal collected guns," he paused and covered his mouth. "I'm sorry if you didn't know that."

"It's quite aware." She was relieved that he actually did know *something* about her son. "I know what he was in to. He still lived at home before everything happened. I found his collection when I cleared out his room."

"Well I met him at a gun shop. He was quite a connoisseur of weapons and things of that nature. And me having recently come back from the army, I was also very familiar."

"You seem a little older than my son." She noticed how versed he was, not to mention he didn't use slang. "He was nineteen when he passed."

"I'm only four years older than him."

"I see," she smiled. "Continue."

"Well we agreed to exchange numbers and from that point on, we remained friends. That is until he started dating that *girl*."

"Who?" she wondered why *any* girl would've ended their friendship.

"Yvonna. She didn't like me very much, and truthfully I didn't care for her."

At this point Caven was forgetting the script he and Yvonna

Reign

rehearsed. If he would've remembered it correctly, he would've *never* mentioned Yvonna's name. She didn't want him learning anything *real* about her past.

"Yeah, she was a spoiled bitch and I never liked her."

"Really? Why do you say that?" although he should not have pried, he was intrigued about Yvonna's past because he worshipped the ground she walked on. And he certainly never thought of her as spoiled.

"Because she was," She sipped her now lukewarm coffee and couldn't wait to trash her name. "When she doesn't get her way, she has a tendency to react. She drove everybody crazy, including that fucking father of hers who killed my son."

"Yvonna's father murdered Bilal?" He asked as if he were surprised. "Why?"

"She said he was having flashbacks of being in the army or some bullshit like that. And they're still looking for him now. And if you ask me, she knows where he is. In all of the years I've known that child, I've never met him once. It's like he only talks to her," she responded shrugging her shoulders. "Whatever's going on, she still doesn't have to be so fuckin' hateful! She wanted me to turn my back on my only grandson just because her best friend is his mother."

"Hold up, Bilal and Yvonna's best friend had a child together?" he asked looking at the boy in the kitchen.

"Yes and that sent her through the roof before she left. We haven't heard from her since."

Now he was really digging himself into a hole. Yvonna would kill him if she knew he was asking questions they hadn't gone over.

One of the things besides the baby that raised a red flag to Caven was the murder of her ex-boyfriend Bilal. Yvonna told him that while her father was cleaning his gun, he shot him by mistake and he was killed instantly. So he wondered why the lies.

"Anyway," he continued getting back on script. "Bilal and I eventually lost contact. It was like he hated me or something. So I left his life, and never returned until now. A mutual friend from the area said he was taking flowers to his grave and I almost fell back. I couldn't believe Bilal was dead. I just thought he didn't want to hear from me." He looked into her eyes and was preparing to lay it on thick because Yvonna didn't want him gone until the tears fell from her eyes. She wanted her world rocked. "And when I heard it was a closed casket funeral I died inside all over again. Nyzon was so beautiful. And now I'm finding out it's all that bitches' father's fault!"

Beautiful? Bernice thought that word was a little misused coming from a man's mouth.

"M…Mr. Boyd," she said trying not to cry. "Please! I have to care for my grandchild now. His mother will be here shortly to pick him up. I'm gonna have to ask you to leave."

"Oh…oh…I'm so sorry." He wiped he actor tears from his face. "I'm being so insensitive. Here I am crying like a baby and he was your son. You should be the one crying. You've probably shed your share of tears though. I'm so pathetic, I should be ashamed."

"Its okay." She stood up and a few tears fell from her eyes. "But I still need you to leave. Now."

Caven remained seated until Bilal Jr. came running into the living room.

"Is that his son?"

"Uh…yes," she said picking him up and holding him on her hip.

"They have the same lips." he said running his index finger gently over the child's mouth.

"Mr. Boyd leave my home!" she demanded as her mouth hung open. *What kind of man would touch a baby that way?*

Everything was clear. At first she had a feeling but now she was positive. Caven was there to imply that he and her son had a sexual relationship. The mere thought of it alone disgusted her.

"I take it you understand what type of friends we were now." He smirked.

"Leave now!" she continued. The tears were coming out of her eyes by the pound…and they were just what Yvonna wanted.

"I'm leaving." He walked toward the door. "But I want to leave some pictures of me and him behind. You deserve to know the truth. *The whole truth.* He was everything to me."

When he pulled the pictures out of the man purse he carried, the first one she saw almost made her drop lil Bilal on the floor. Instead, she placed him down and snatched the pictures out of his hands.

The first *doctored* picture was of Bilal and Caven kissing in a hotel bed. The second was of Bilal and Caven hugging one another. She released the grip she had on the photos and watched them float to the floor. The pictures were real, but the face in them was not. They paid to have Bilal's face entered by some professionals, where Caven's ex-lover's face used to be. Yes, Caven had a thing for men, at least before he met Yvonna. But if Bernice would've looked harder at the photos, she would've noticed the body in the pictures didn't belong to her son. Instead, she looked only at his face. *Smack! Smack! Smack!*

"How dare you try to destroy my son's name! Leave now before I call the cops."

"I deserved that," he said holding his face. "But you deserved the truth."

"Get out!" she screamed pointing at the door.

"I am." He said slyly stealing one last look at his child. "But you may see me again, when he gets a little older. I'm interested in seeing how much *alike*, they really are."

When he succeeded at getting her to doubt her son, he walked out the door, and ruined her life.

Mission accomplished.

Chapter Fourteen

For The Sake Of Control

Laughter and satisfaction was heavy between them. "Are you sure she was crying?" Yvonna questioned in the hotel room they shared at the Embassy Suites in Washington, D.C.

"I'm positive. I would've stayed longer to mush her face in it some more but she threw me out."

"That's perfect!" Yvonna jumped around wearing a tiny pair of blue jean shorts by Beyonce's *House of Dereon* collection. She was also wearing a ripped up plain wife beater. "You're sure she didn't have a clue I was in on it?"

"Positive," he laughed remembering briefly mentioning her name.

"You were great!" She slowly approached him where he sat on the couch. She was preparing to use sex as a reward and a form of mind control. After all, it was because of him she'd be able to cross Bernice Santana's name off the list.

"Can I ask you something?"

"Sure." She found her way to her knees to unfasten his pants. "What is it?" Taking him into her mouth, she was giving him the "Crucial" head job.

"Mmmmmm." He moaned. "It's a question about your life." He said looking down on her. She stopped sucking his dick. "It seems like there's so much about you I don't know." She stood up and sat next to him on the sofa wiping her mouth and he adjusted his pants.

"Why you ask me that? Were ya'll talkin'about me or something?"

"No," he smiled. "I did everything you ask me-,"

"So why does it seem like I'm not telling you everything?" She interrupted. *Is he betraying me too?* She thought. *Do I have to add his name to my list?* Her head was hurting and she started to feel lightheaded. "You know as much about me as I want you to know."

"Well," he said walking away from her hoping to prevent what happened many times before when she got mad. "It's just that," he hesitated. "I made a mistake of saying your name. And she mentioned Bilal had a baby with your best friend. Is that true?"

"What the fuck?!" she said stomping off now enveloped in anger. "Why didn't you stick to the plan?! Why you have to talk about stuff we didn't discuss?!"

"I forgot. I'm sorry." He tried to calm her down but it was too late.

"So you turnin' on me too huh?" She questioned her forehead filled with lines.

"No," he pleaded. "I wouldn't-."

Before he could finish his sentence she smacked him in his face. All she could think about was him stabbing her in the back like so many others in her life. She was no longer rational. She was no longer sane.

~~~~~~

Yvonna was laid on the floor her arms outstretched at her sides. When she came to, the room was a mess. The books which held the hotel information was scattered everywhere and a few of the pages were torn and thrown about the floor. Clothes were out of the dresser and things were in total disarray.

"Everything's fine," Caven told the hotel personnel as he talked to him in the hallway with the door slightly open. "Thanks for stopping by."

"Well please keep it down," the short white security guard advised. "We had a lot of complaints about this room. Somebody said they heard a lot of commotion." He was trying to look inside but Caven blocked his view.

"Like I said," Caven repeated. "Everything's fine now."

When he closed the door, Yvonna held her head and sat on the couch. All of the rooms at the Embassy had a bedroom, and private area for the living room.

"What just happened?" she asked the taste in her mouth thick and bitter.

"Nothing." He was short but not angry considering there was a small gash on the left side of his head dripping with blood. "Get some rest. I'll clean this up."

"I hurt you again didn't I?"

"Lay down, baby." He smiled. "I'm okay."

"I'm so sorry," she said running over to him pulling his body to hers. "I'll never do it again."

"I know, Yvonna." He lifted her tiny body from the floor and carried her in his arms. "I just want you to get some rest." Once he placed her in the bed, he tucked her arms under the covers as if she was a rag doll.

"Let me take care of you," he said as a drop of his blood splattered on the burgundy comforter.

"I'm so sorry." She reached over to the nightstand to grab a white napkin. "I don't know why you put up with me."

"I'm fine, Yvonna. I'm more concerned about you." "Are you sure?" she asked wiping his blood with the napkin.

"Positive," he smiled. "Now get some sleep."

"I love you Caven." she lied.

"I know." He hoped.

"I need you too." That part was true. "I hope you realize it."

"I do, now get some sleep."

With that he diligently cleaned the room and she drifted off to sleep. It wasn't the first time she went off, and it most certainly wouldn't be the last.

Chapter Fifteen

The Fall Of Another

The rush of people entering and leaving the grocery store was at an all time high.

Yvonna stood in line and glanced at her diamond studded Rolex watch. *Shit! I'm gonna be late!* She thought as she anxiously beat her feet on the floor. She picked up a magazine with Jay-Z on the cover hoping it would keep her attention.

But as she thumbed through the Vibe magazine, she quickly realized it wasn't working. Looking ahead, she counted five people before she could even place the apple pie, and vanilla ice cream she purchased on the counter.

Five minutes later she heard, "Just one more minute, mam," the Safeway clerk advised the person directly in front of Yvonna. "The customer went to grab some milk."

Great! Finally I make it up here and somebody's holding up the line!

"That's alright," the black woman in her early forties replied. "I'm busy reading this anyway," she said referring to the Essence magazine she was holding. "I can't get over how good Janet looks."

Well try bitch! Yvonna thought.

"She does look good doesn't she? I can't believe how much weight she's lost."

As they carried on frivolous conversations, Yvonna was growing weary. *These bitches bout to make me swell on they asses.* She had told Cream she'd make it to her apartment in Bowie by eight and it was already nine.

"I don't mean to be rude," Yvonna lied. "But uh…it looks like she went shopping for more than just milk, and to be honest, I'm sick of waiting. Can we move the line along please?"

"Okay," the clerk responded uncomfortable with Yvonna's combativeness. "It's just that she's pregnant and I figured she was taking a little more time getting back because of her condition, but no worries," she continued ringing the next customer's first item. "I'll get started now."

When the clerk was prepared to ring the next item on the belt, a swollen pregnant woman rushed passed Yvonna to the counter. Waiving milk in hand, she made her presence known.

"Ahn Ahn ya'll! I was next," she screamed pushing her big belly against Yvonna and the lady before her. "I told you I was comin' right back, Miss."

"It's okay," the clerk smiled. "You can go after I ring her up."

"No the hell she can't either!" Yvonna advised. "This bitch went on a second shopping spree and I'll be damn if I'm gonna wait a minute longer."

"You can ring her before me," the lady said pushing her items back. "I'll wait."

"You sure?" the clerk asked.

"Positive."

The clerk voided the items and rung up the pregnant lady's milk.

"Thanks, Miss lady," the ghetto girl said eye balling Yvonna because of her comment. "I preciate it."

"No problem."

Yvonna sighed and was ready to smack all of them, including the clerk. She hated grocery stores and this was reason number one. Everybody was worried about themselves without regard for what others had to do.

"You better than me," Yvonna told the lady with much attitude.

"Why you say that?"

"Cuz she would not have gotten back in front of me. I don't care if she's pregnant or not." She was loud enough for the girl to hear her. She wanted her to say something. Always a fighter, she would've dropped that pie on the floor for a chance to whip her ass. Pregnant or not.

"You need to be patient, honey. Life will have you in a hurry if you let it."

"Whatever," Yvonna said brushing her wise words off. "I control life, it doesn't control me." With that she smoothed the back of her hair with her hands and looked inside her new Marc Jacob purse for her money.

"You need God in your *life*. Or you won't have one." The woman looked into her eyes.

"You have your people, and I have mine." Yvonna spit words of venom. "God never answered my prayers before so I stopped talking to him a long time ago."

"I'm ready for you, miss," the clerk advised waking the lady from the hurtful words Yvonna had just given her to swallow.

"Oh...," she said looking at the clerk and then back at Yvonna. "You go ahead, young lady. You need to get to where you're going quick...and I don't want to stand in your way."

Yvonna rushed past her without offering the woman a chance to change her mind. She had one plan and one plan only. Getting revenge, and nothing or nobody else would stand in her way. Not even God.

~~~~~~

When Cream opened the door and saw Yvonna standing behind it, she dropped the kitchen towel she had in her hand to hug her. Gripping her neck, she cried when she saw her face.

"I missed you Yvonna," she continued holding her tight. "I missed you soo much!"

"I missed you too," she smiled realizing her plan would be easier than she thought.

After the greetings were over, Yvonna washed her hands and made herself comfortable in Cream 's kitchen.

"I love your place!" Yvonna yelled. Everything was bright and colorful and it expressed Cream's personality to a "T". She had the entire Ikea collection in her apartment. Beautiful colors and contemporary furniture filled it. "I see you still have taste."

"Not like you," Cream said still looking upon her friend with admiration. "I wish I did though."

Over the years, Cream had become even more beautiful. She now had blonde shoulder length hair and appeared to be glowing. Yvonna could tell by the white Dior shoes she was sporting along with her linen Ella Moss short set that life was treating her well. Her makeup was light and she resembled Jessica Simpson.

"So what's been up?" Cream asked as she sliced the vegetable lasagna she took from the oven. "Tell me everything and don't hold back shit!"

"Okay!" she laughed. "I'm engaged to a-,"

"Hold up!" Cream screamed dropping her oven mitt to the floor. "Did you say engaged?"

"Yes!"

"I'm so happy for you!" she jumped up and down.

Her fakeness was so sickening that Yvonna wanted to punch her in the stomach. She wondered how she could be happy for her when for real, she stabbed her in the back four years earlier. *Everything in time. I'll give this fake bitch exactly what she deserves.*

"Thanks, girl! He loves me and if everything works out, I'll be having some Milan babies in the near future."

"Hold up," she paused from placing the plates on the table. Everything she did had to be grand, including her statements. "He's white?!"

"Yep! Well...white and black mixed."

"I can't believe Yvonna took a step on the wild side," she laughed taking a break from her antics to sip from her glass of wine. "I knew you'd find somebody."

It was too late, the words had slipped out just as easy as she said them and somewhat spoiled the mood.

"What do you mean, Cream? You thought my life was over just because of what Bilal did to me?"

"No," Cream responded shaking her head. "It's just that... when you left, and nobody heard from you, we thought it was because of Bilal or that Sabrina had Bilal Jr."

"Oh...so she named him after Bilal?"

She nodded yes.

"Well just so you know, I'm fine," she responded placing the salad on the table. "I left to get my mind straight that's all."

"I understand," Cream said choosing her words carefully. "You look good though."

And she was right. Yvonna was killing the Seven jeans and the white corset she chose to wear with it.

"Thanks," she winked "But I already know."

"Still cocky too!"

"Shut up, girl," Yvonna responded nudging her arm exposing the seven carat custom made ring Terrell had given to her. "You know you like when I keep it real wit' your ass."

Later they looked at some old photos and Cream showed Yvonna her purse collection. She had a Kooba Paige shoulder bag, a couple of Dior Gaucho purses and some Gucci Brit medium hobo joints. Yvonna appreciated her label game but thought it couldn't compare to hers. After they talked about old times, Yvonna ran through her head how quickly it would take her plan to fall into place.

Prior to finding out that Cream was no good, both of them were tight. Cream was the only white girl in the neighborhood because her mother sold her to a neighbor for some dope when she was just three years old. When the dealer realized a baby didn't fit into his plans, he left her on a church doorstep and another woman took her into her home. The black church going woman raised her as best as she could but once the streets got a hold of her, it was a wrap.

When Cream was sixteen, she became too hard to control and the woman began to let her do whatever she wanted. Sabrina and Yvonna took her under their wing after being tired of seeing her getting her ass beat by the neighborhood girls. But it was Yvonna, who treated her like a sister. Whenever Yvonna thought about all the things she did for her, she became furious.

"I want to ask you something," Yvonna said turning around to face her on the black leather sofa. Before saying a word, she grabbed the remote and hit mute on the 54 inch plasma TV on Cream's wall.

"Shoot!"

"Did you really miss me?" Yvonna sounded sincere. She already knew out of everybody, Cream was devastated when she left. She just wanted to hear it.

"Did I miss you," she said turning around to face her. "You were my best friend. Don't get me wrong, me and Sabrina are close, but we were always closer. I am sooo sorry for my part in everything. I shoulda told you but I didn't know how. I felt caught in the middle. If I said something to you, Sabrina would hate me. And if I didn't say anything, you would hate me. What was I supposed to do?"

"You know you're the only one I thought about when I left right?"

"Awww," she said hitting her on the leg. "I thought about you too. It wasn't just me, Sabrina cried when you left. And for months Dave would ask me if I heard from you. He stopped asking after awhile but I could tell he still wanted to know. So when I saw him, I'd tell him straight up that I hadn't heard from you so he wouldn't have to ask me."

"Sabrina and Dave huh?" Yvonna said their names out loud and they tasted like shit in her mouth. "Why were they asking about me?"

"Well Sabrina figured your leaving was all her fault and Dave felt fucked up for making you get into that car. He's changed a little. I mean, he's still the same thug but he's different. He don't get involved in a lot of stuff no more."

"So I've been told," she blurt out by accident.

"Oh…you've seen him already?"

"Uh…no," she smiled. "I just heard some things about him that's all."

"I think he has a crush on you or something," Cream advised.

"Not interested."

"I know," she said focusing on her hands.

"But maybe I'll stop by to see him and Sabrina later. To be

honest, I'm not trippin' off of that stuff anymore. We were kids and as you can see, I'm a woman now. I believe in letting bygones be bygones."

"That's good," Cream smiled.

"So what have you been doing with yourself? Are you happy?"

"Yes," she smiled as she went away mentally before returning with a glaze on her face. "I'm *very* happy. You know me and Avante are finally getting married."

"No I didn't," she lied again. The private detective gave her everything she needed to know about them. "Congratulations on your upcoming nuptials. Here I am spilling my shit out, and you're about to become a wife too."

"I can't believe it." She blushed.

"Now do you have a job or is he taking care of you?"

"It's all him. He got into the FBI and is making good money. We are closing on a house in Bowie next month. I'm so happy Yvonna," she said getting excited. "Even more so that you're back."

"And why is that?"

"Because now you can be in my wedding."

"Maybe," Yvonna responded, brushing the side of Cream's face with her hand. "Maybe."

Cream was so excited by her touch that she stood up.

"Can I get you something else to drink?" She looked rattled.

"No," Yvonna giggled. She knew she was crushing on her even if Cream didn't know. "I'm okay."

"Well let me get myself something then."

"Sure," Yvonna said hunching her shoulders. "Whatever you need."

The reaction she got when she touched her proved what she already knew. Cream was still sweet on her, and had been since the Southeast days. All Yvonna had to do now was find out how sweet on her she actually was. When she returned she sat on the far end of the sofa.

"Why are you all the way over there?"

"Oh…uh…no reason."

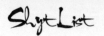

"Well move closer girl," Yvonna demanded. "I haven't seen you in years and here you are acting like you don't even know me."

"That's not true," she said moving only a few spaces closer. "It's just that," she paused. "I'm really happy you're here."

"I can't tell."

"What do you want me to do to prove it?" Cream questioned.

"Show me."

"Show you? Show you how?"

"You can think of something," Yvonna advised moving over to her. Without waiting on an answer, she tilted her head like she was coming in for a kiss when Avante walked in the door.

Both of them rose to their feet, and looked as if they were up to something. Yvonna hadn't realized he lived in the same apartment, the investigator failed to let her know that, otherwise she would've planned another route to get back at her. At first her intentions were to ruin her relationship, by making Cream feel she was in love with her. And when she fell deep, she'd break her heart and relationship. But after seeing Avante, she had something better in mind and it would consist of a third party.

Chapter Sixteen

Sorry

Craven's snores were faint as Yvonna waited for her aunt's response on the phone.

"Yvonna," Jhane breathed heavily returning to the phone. "She said she's not ready."

"But she's my sister," Yvonna said slipping into one of her brown Fendi sandals, followed by the next one. She hopped on one foot until both were on. She stood up straight and looked into the mirror. "I deserve to know how she's doing."

"Yvonna…she got the money you've been sending her okay? I know she's grateful and I am too because I ain't got no help around here. But Jesse doesn't want to see you right now and I'm not going to make her."

Yvonna gave herself the look of approval in the mirror. She'd spent ten thousand dollars alone purchasing new clothes to look sexy during her stay in D.C. Her new thing was rocking Beyonce's clothing line. She was into that rustic shit. So she wore a cream top and jeans that hung off her hip bone. She'd moussed and dyed her hair last night so it was shiny jet black. As always, she killed them with the dark "Persona" eye shadow by MAC.

"What about the letters I've written her over the years. Has she gotten any of them?" she asked turning around in the mirror eyeing her round plump ass.

"Yes."

"And?" she said checking her lip gloss and makeup one more time. "Did she say anything? Give you any messages for me?"

"Like I said, when she's ready to contact you she will. But you can't keep calling here expectin' her to answer the phone."

"She's my damn sister!"

"And you're fuckin' spoiled!" Jhane yelled back. "If you weren't such a spoiled crazy bitch, you woulda never left her here to begin with. Now bye!"

"Crash!"

Yvonna threw the phone against the hotel wall startling Caven out of a deep sleep. He jumped up fearing she was having one of her episodes again.

"Uh…everything alright?" he asked standing straight up against the wall, prepared to duck if he had to.

"No! My fuckin' aunt's keepin' me away from my sister!"

"For what?"

"I don't know! I think they're brainwashing her or something."

"So what you gonna do?"

"I can't think about that now but I'm gettin' my sister out of there," she said as she tried to brush things off to prepare for her day. "Get dressed," she continued as she grabbed the mousse can once more to smooth the back of her hair down again. "I need you to take me to Greenbelt Park. I'm meeting Cream and Sabrina there later on."

"Are you sure you're going to be able to handle this by yourself?"

"Of course," she winked. "Everything's falling into place."

"I'm glad they're getting what they deserve for killing your mother."

That was the first time she'd heard her lie out loud. She convinced Caven into believing that Cream, Sabrina and Dave were all members of the YBM, and burned her house down killing her mother. Although the lie was ridiculous considering at one point they were all friends, Caven didn't question her, for fear of Yvonna going off.

Yvonna *did* tell him that she was angry with Bernice for concealing the fact that Bilal had a baby behind her back. But Caven didn't know a best friend was involved until he visited her. Yvonna's lies were all over the place, and she knew at some point, they'd catch up with her.

She thought telling him the truth about her motives for revenge wouldn't give him enough reason to help. So she told lie on top of lie.

"I'm happy I'm getting them back too," she said wrapping her arms around his neck before kissing him gently on the lips. "Finally."

~~~~~~

The sun was beaming on the park and there was a feeling of summer madness in the air. Sabrina was hugging Yvonna's tiny body so tightly that for a second, she got lost in the mounds of flesh she'd carried around all these years. Her cheap perfume was sickening and if she held her much longer, Yvonna was sure she'd be sick.

"You look so pretty," Sabrina smiled squeezing Yvonna again before pushing her back to look at her. "Doesn't she, Cream?"

"Yes," she said spreading the thick grey quilt over the grass. "I told her last week when I saw her."

Just then Bilal, Jr. walked up and grabbed his mother's leg.

"Mommy…mommy, mommy," he continued not giving her time to answer. "I want another hot dog."

"Girl this boy gonna eat me out of house and home," she said looking down at him.

I doubt that very seriously. Yvonna thought.

"Shannon!" Sabrina yelled over Yvonna's head. "Get this boy another hot dog. As a matter of fact, get him three cuz he's gonna be askin' me for another one in a minute anyway! And bring me two! Damn that boy can eat!" she giggled.

The short light skin girl scooped Bilal Jr. up and took him to the table where the food was spread out. Cream, Sabrina and Yvonna sat on the quilt pretending as if everything was as it had been before the violation of their friendship.

"I'm so happy you forgave me Yvonna," Sabrina said as she took off her shoes and spread her short, fat stubby toes. Yvonna was grossed out at the sight, and if she was hungry before, she wasn't now.

"I ain't trippin' no more," she said lying on her back squinting her eyes at the sun. "I'm a woman and pretty soon, I'ma have my own family with my new husband."

"I heard," Sabrina said nudging her like she did back in the day. "You bout to be a married woman!"

"I know if Yvonna's marrying him," Cream said lying next to Yvonna face up. "He has to be fine."

"Do tell," Sabrina responded. "We have a lot of catching up to do after four years so don't leave nothing out."

This bitch has a fucking nerve. If I really was marrying some-body else, I don't know why she would think I'd tell her backstab-bing ass! She's lucky I don't punch her in the fucking nose right now.

"Well he's half white, black and Indian. He's kinda tall and he loves me to death. He has his own practice –,"

"Wait," Sabrina said interrupting her. "He's a doctor?"

"Yep, and a good one at that," Yvonna continued fanning the pesty fly away from her face.

"How you land his ass?" Sabrina asked.

What the fuck that's suppose to mean? Yvonna thought.

"I use to work for him at first," she responded still salty about her question. "But after awhile," she smiled. "We just realized that there was more between us."

"So where do you guys live?" Cream responded.

"Not around here."

"Oh…," Sabrina said sensing she didn't want to give her any details. "What hotel are you staying in now?"

"It's in D.C., why?"

"Yvonna, I'm not trying to pry," she said in a sweet tone. "I was only asking because I didn't want you spending so much money if you didn't have too. Cream said you're planning on being in town for awhile."

"I'll be fine. I don't want for anything."

"The reason I asked," she continued clearing her throat. "Was because I wanted you to know that you're more than welcome to stay with me and Bilal Jr.. I would love to have you around. You know I can still cook girl and I don't mind taking care of you. Actually, it would make me feel better if you let me take care of you while you're in town."

Yvonna was prepared to say no until she saw how much easier it would be to destroy her life from the inside.

"On second thought," Yvonna smiled before leaning over to hug her. "I would love to stay with you, especially with me staying around a little longer to help this girl plan for her wedding," she continued tapping Cream.

"I really appreciate it too! And if I can return the favor for you and your wedding, just let me know." Cream smiled just thinking about how happy she'd be to finally marry Avante.

"It's the least the maid of honor can do," Yvonna replied sipping on her soda.

"Maid of honor?" Sabrina said carefully to be sure she heard her correctly.

"Yes," Cream said giving her the *look*. "I decided I wanted Yvonna to be my maid of honor, considering she's back now. You understand right?"

The look on Sabrina's face said it all. Hell no she didn't agree but she decided not to express her feelings about it. At least not now anyway. What Sabrina didn't know was that Cream hated the idea of her big body standing next to her, blocking her view at the wedding. Sexy ass Yvonna would definitely be an addition to the wedding photos.

"I understand girl," she smiled. "As long as I'm in it, it don't even matter to me."

The women went on and on with small conversation until Dave walked up on them. Yvonna almost passed out when she saw how handsome he was. He allowed a five o'clock shadow to cover his face and the white cut off T-shirt he wore showed his muscular arms covered with tattoos. His smile was so bright that Yvonna had to turn away the moment he flashed it at her.

"Hey stranger," he said making himself comfortable on the comforter they shared.

"H…hey," Yvonna smiled back.

"They told me you were back in town so I had to check you out," he continued looking her up and down. "It's nice to see you found your way back home punk. I was bout to send a search party to come look for you."

Yvonna was at a lost for words. Up until this point, the game was being played as planned. She didn't know what she expected, but she damn sure didn't think Dave would look so good. And after only four years.

"It's nice to see you too," she said trying to appear un-phased by his presence. "Crazy Dave."

"Naw, shawty," he corrected her. "That's not what they call me anymore. I'm just Dave now."

"Yeah," Cream interrupted. "He's nothing like he used to be. He hardly got time for us anymore," she continued. "He wasn't even gonna come out today until we told him you were here."

"That ain't even true," he smiled. "I hang out wit ya'll all the time."

"When, boy?" Sabrina asked. "Last time I saw you was when we went to Bilal's grave - ," Sabrina stopped realizing she was treading on thin ice. "Sorry, Yvonna," Sabrina said under her breath.

"Look! I'm over Bilal okay? So if you worried about not being able to talk about him around me, don't!"

"You're right," Sabrina said softly.

"Can I talk to you alone Yvonna?" Dave asked removing her from the tension.

"Uh…sure," she said as he helped her stand up.

"And don't try hitting on her either," Cream interjected. "She's engaged."

He ignored her as they walked off.

"So how's life?" he chose to ask first.

"Good," she responded dusting off the back of her pants. Had she known he was showing up right then and there, she would've checked her makeup.

"I can see that," he laughed looking her up and down.

"So you're corny now too huh?"

"Naw, I'm just tryin' to break the ice that's all."

"Well break it by telling me what the real deal is."

They stopped walking and he stood directly in front of her. His eyes piercing into her soul. The mint on his breath was faint but strong enough to add a plus to an already perfect man standing before her.

"Look, I'm sorry about what happened in the car that night. I shoulda never made you come with me."

"You call that an apology?" she questioned fanning a bee which flew in front of her face. The bugs were getting on her fucking nerves.

"Actually I do. I was a stupid nigga back then Yvonna, and I didn't have my head on straight."

"And what do you call yourself now?"

"A changed man," he said gently grabbing her hand which hung down by her side.

She held on to his touch just a moment longer before snatching away from him and folding her hands across her chest.

"It don't seem like you changed too much to me," she said taking two steps away. "You still pushy."

"You think?" he said placing his hands in his back pockets.

"I know," she smiled. "Anyway, you came in time to hear the news so you already know." she continued. "I'm getting married."

"I heard Cream when I walked up." He was frowning and didn't even know it. "So I guess you two are happy then?" he asked as the glare from his watch hit her eyes.

"Yeah, we are."

"Well I'm happy for you too."

"Great!" she said wondering why he appeared to have some unseen control over her. "You know everything about my life, and I know nothing about yours."

"That's because I'm more interested in you."

"Oh really?"

"Yeah…really." The way he said it, got Yvonna's pussy jumping. For a moment she wondered what it would be like to fuck him and then her mind went into overtime.

What the fuck am I doing? Why am I allowing him to enter my head?

"Well you don't need to be concerned about my life because I'm good," she advised.

"Can I have a hug?" he asked.

Those four schoolboy words worked her over more than anything she could imagine.

"I guess so." She responded falling into his chest. She felt his heart beat and his muscular arms wrapped her up like a goose down comforter. She exhaled out loud before dusting herself off.

"Now can we get back to Cream and them?"

"Sure. But just so you know, you gonna be mine."

"So you're finally admitting you like me."

He laughed.

"But have you forgotten? I'm not your type remember?"

Before he could respond, they heard a screaming female's voice. Both of them turned around to see Cream being pummeled by a dark skin girl wearing jean shorts, a black T-shirt and no shoes. Not only was she beating Cream unmercifully, she had her in a head lock using her thighs to hold her face as she unleashed on her.

"Stop it!! Please stop!" Cream called out.

"Bitch, ain't no body gonna stop me from beatin' dis ass! I been tryin' to catch up wit' your white ass for a minute and now I finally got you!" After the crazed girl told her how badly she wanted to kick her ass, she followed up with blow after blow. By the time Dave was able to reach the scene, Cream 's face was completely bludgeoned.

"Fuck wrong wit you girl?" he asked whisking her up as if she weighed five pounds.

"Get the fuck off me, Dave!" she continued swinging wildly, still unable to release herself from his hold. "This, bitch stole my husband and don't even want him seein' his kids! Fuck kinda woman is she?"

It was then that Yvonna realized it was Treyana. Instead of

approaching the scene as quickly as Dave did, she played the background hoping she'd get away again and commence to beating Cream's ass some more. It took everything in her power not to crown Treyana because she was able to do something she couldn't. At least not now anyway.

"What's going on?" Yvonna eventually asked approaching the two. Cream was sobbing and holding her face.

"I finally got a chance to kick dis bitch's ass that's what's goin on!" She said pointing. Treyana was trying to get away from Dave but he kept the hold he had on her.

"You need to take that up wit main man," Dave advised as he finally released her but kept close watch of her. "But I ain't bout to have you out here fightin' this girl"

"You ain't got shit to do wit' it Dave," Treyana said putting her shoes on her dusty feet. "I don't know why you won't just let me handle my biz."

"What's going on?" Sabrina asked waddling over to the scene minutes later. Yvonna wasn't sure, but she believed she approached the scene late on purpose too. After all, she had just gotten the news that she wasn't the maid of honor and that Yvonna was. "You okay, Cream?" she asked as she held her looking back at Treyana for answers.

Nobody responded. Cream just got herself together and ran to her car as Dave made sure she got there safe. He was so caught up into the bullshit, that he didn't bother saying goodbye to Yvonna. Sabrina followed and suddenly Treyana and Yvonna were left alone.

"Fuckin', bitch!" Treyana grumbled. "I'ma beat her ass everyday of the week and twice on Sundays!"

"Hold up," Yvonna said catching her before she walked off.

"What you want?" she asked grabbing her purse off the ground. "I thought you were locked up or somethin'!"

"Why would I be locked up?" Yvonna huffed.

"The cops been askin' for you and could neva find yo father! That's why!"

"Well I'm not hidin' so if they want me, they can find me,"

Yvonna responded brushing the comment off. "But look…I want to help you."

"Help me with what?" she said walking away from her.

"Help you get what you want," Yvonna responded catching up to her again.

"I don't need help doin' nothin'. I can hold my own."

"I don't doubt that. But what if I tell you I'ma help you get back with Avante?"

Suddenly Treyana's frowns were gone and she looked open to hearing what Yvonna had to say.

"And how do you plan on doin' that?" She asked as she stopped walking.

"You got to trust me first," Yvonna said wrapping her arm around her neck while walking with her again.

"Trust you?" she said pulling away from her hold. "What you some kinda dyke or somethin'? Cuz I don't get down like that!"

"What are you talkin' about?" she asked happy she pulled away anyway. Her underarms were so strong that Yvonna wondered if she even bothered to wash them within the past few days. "I'm talkin' about getting you back with your husband! Ain't nobody hittin' on your dust-," She cut herself short. She was about to give her a piece of her mind but she thought better of it. "Listen, I want to see ya'll back together."

"How you know I wanna be back wit him anyway?"

"Why you out here doin' all this if you don't want to be wit him?"

"Cuz he need to take care of his kids and every time they call his house, that bitch tells them he busy! He got two kids and she don't want him to eva see 'em! I'm sick of her ass! She ruined my fuckin' life!"

"See…," Yvonna said in a low voice. "I can tell you want to be with him. Like you said, he deserves to see his kids without Cream getting in the way. I can help you make it happen."

"Don't get it twisted. I .don't want nothin' to do with his bum ass."

"Treyana please! You out here stompin' a bitch out five years after he left you cuz you miss him," she said tapping her arm. "I remember how tight ya'll were. Don't forget, we lived in the same building. To be honest, I kinda feel responsible since she was my friend. If I didn't have her over, Avante would've never saw her."

Treyana looked at Yvonna as if she thought about whipping her ass now. Because she knew what she said was true. But when Yvonna gave her the look like, *You Don't Want It With Me Bitch*, Treyana softened up. "It ain't right that Cream took your man, and here they are bout to get married. How he even get you to sign the divorce papers?"

"He told me they were papers for life insurance."

"You ain't read 'em first?"

She shook her head no.

"Well...fuck that...ya'll deserve to be together."

"I thought ya'll were friends?" Treyana asked. "So why you helpin' me?"

"We *were* friends. But right is right and wrong is wrong. I want to see a family back together not ripped apart. Now do you want my help or not?"

Treyana looked into her eyes trying to figure her out. The longer she waited, the more Yvonna knew she had her.

"What I got to do?"

"Just do everything I say and you'll be back with him in no time. I promise."

Chapter Seventeen

Surprise!

Yvonna was propped up on Treyana's new sofa talking to a hysterical Cream on the phone. She was paying more attention to the design on her toes done by the only black Chinese woman she ever met, than she was to her upset friend.

"Listen, you have to calm down," Yvonna said rubbing her fingers over the freshly dried red nail polish. "It's not that serious."

"But I don't know how to calm down!"

Yvonna rolled her eyes.

"What if he thinks I'm doing something behind his back Yvonna? I would die if he doesn't want to marry me."

"You asked for my help and I'm giving it to you. All men, and I do mean *all* men like their space. And if you take that from them, they'll stray," she said sitting up straight on the sofa to sip from the "Full Throttle" energy drink on the new glass table. "Besides, this is just to prove to him that you aren't like some of these women out here, who don't allow their men to breathe. Trust me Cream, he'll love you for this."

"But…but..,"

"But, but, nothing, Cream! Now if you want to crowd him every five minutes then so be it, but don't be surprised when he leaves you like he left Treyana."

There was brief silence until Treyana yelled from the bathroom, "Yvonna! Can you call Patience for me and check on my kids?"

Yvonna tried to muffle her voice by placing her hands over the receiving part of the phone, but she was sure Cream heard Treyana's voice.

"Who was that?" Cream asked in between sniffles.

"Nobody," she said wanting to pimp slap Treyana for being so ghetto. She knew Cream would die if she knew she was betraying her by hanging over Treyana's apartment. "Just do as I say, and I'll call you back later." Yvonna said blowing her off. "And don't worry, everything will go great tonight and Avante will be able to see how much you love him."

Without giving Cream a chance to respond, she hung up and walked to the kitchen. There on the refrigerator she saw the number for Patience, Treyana's ghetto ass babysitter. She hated looking at her, let alone saying two words to her over the phone.

"Boy you betta bring my car back and stop playin' with me!" Yelled the voice on the other end of the phone when the number was dialed.

"Hello?!" Yvonna said wondering who she thought she was.

"Oh...who dis?"

"It's Yvonna, Patience. I'm just calling to check on Treyana's kids."

"Girl, you prob-lee think I'm lunchin'!" She screamed. "That tired ass man of mine took my car and now I ain't got nobody to take me to the store to cash in my fuckin' WIC. Plus I needed to get some food wit' my Independence Card," she continued as if Yvonna gave a fuck.

"Oh," Yvonna responded. She could care less. All she was doing was putting in a call like Treyana asked her to. "Uh...well, I hope you get it back soon. Anyway, how are the kids?"

"Them bad ass mothafuckas aight girl! They over here eatin' some cereal wit' my kids now."

"At seven o'clock at night?"

"Yeah, girl! My kids eat cereal for breakfast, lunch and dinna! Shoooot, food is food."

"Whatever you say," she said wanting to end the call with the ghetto ass bitch. "I'll have Treyana call you back later."

"Aight!"

When she hung up, she was about to ask Treyana was she finished in the bathroom until someone knocked at the front door.

"Now what?" she yelled out loud. "Who is it?" she continued swinging the door open. When she saw who it was she almost fell back.

"How are you sweetheart?"

"Dad?" Sticking her head out the door, she looked in the piss smelly hallway, to see if anyone saw him come in. It was empty.

"I heard you were in the neighborhood so I decided to stop by."

"Well...uh...I don't want to speak to you," she continued sticking her head back in the door, before looking behind her to be sure Treyana wasn't there.

"I understand, sweetheart. I just wanted to tell you I was sorry about what happened to Bilal, and I want you to forgive me."

"Well I can't forgive you! You got the cops looking for me right now behind your shit."

"I don't expect you to forgive me right now sweetheart, but do you think we can ever get past this? Maybe in the future? I've been taking my medicine and I think its working."

She glanced over him and noticed he was wearing the same thing he always did. The brown corduroys with his dark green sweater.

"I don't know," she continued hoping Treyana wouldn't walk out and see him there. "But I gotta go. I'll talk to you later."

"Are you sure?"

"Yes I'm sure," she continued irritated by his pushiness. "But you have to let me get in contact with you. Don't pop up on me like this daddy."

"Okay," he smiled. "You know where to find me?"

"Who are you talkin' to girl?" Treyana asked from behind her. Slam!

"What is wrong with you?" Treyana continued after seeing the door slam shut. The picture with her peasy headed kids fell off the wall and Yvonna picked it back up.

"Nothin'...uh...you ready?"

"Yes, but who was at my door?"

"A friend. An old friend," Yvonna responded walking away from the door hoping she'd follow her and not look out of it.

"I didn't see anybody when the door was open."

Good. Yvonna thought.

"I know," she responded trying to get off the subject. "They had to go in a hurry."

"Girl, you still as crazy as you were when you use to live round here."

"Don't call me that shit again!" Yvonna said as she stepped up to her.

"Aight…aight," Treyana said backing up. "I was just fuckin' wit' you anyway."

"Well I don't fuckin' play like that!" Yvonna advised.

Yvonna was still staring her down. If there was one thing she hated, it was to be called crazy. All her life people used the word "crazy" as a way to describe her actions. One time she hit one of her school mates so hard in the mouth with a pad lock for calling her crazy, she had to get a full set of false teeth. It was her mother who started her hate for the word. She called her crazy whenever she saw her doing things that weren't normal. And Yvonna worked so hard to prove she wasn't, that she hated when people called her that.

"Yvonna?" Treyana looked frightened as she stared her down. "I'm just playing for real. I'm sorry."

What woke her out of the trance was the smell of Treyana's body. For somebody just getting out of the shower, she smelled atrocious. "You did say you washed up right?" Yvonna asked.

"Yeah."

"Well why can I *still* smell your underarms?"

Treyana, with the towel still wrapped around her petite frame, raised her right arm slightly, bent her head down, and took a whiff of her own body.

"I don't smell nothin'."

Yvonna wasn't surprised. She stunk so bad all the time, that she probably thought it was natural.

"Well I smell you,' she said.

"Well I *am* clean!" she said plopping on the couch.

"Show me what you do."

"Do for what?"

"When you wash up," Yvonna said with her hands on her hips.

"Are you cra..," she was about to make a mistake of calling her *crazy* again but didn't. "I'm not doing that."

Yvonna irritated by her combativeness said, "You want me to help you get Avante back right?"

"Yes."

"Okay…well if you can't even do a simple thing like wash your ass properly, how do you think that'll work?"

"Well Avante never had a problem before."

"Are you sure?" She questioned looking around her apartment. "Because I don't recall seeing him here."

Treyana remained seated on the couch for a few more seconds. Rising to her feet, she moved toward the now clean hallway in the direction of the bathroom. Prior to Yvonna coming over and spending over eight thousand dollars on new furniture, new clothes, and a massive cleaning crew, her small D.C. apartment was a hot ass mess. But with Yvonna's help, the apartment was better than presentable. It was fly. She had dark warm colors throughout. She even spent money on painters to repaint the walls. And when the landlord came by to fix the sink, he was shocked that her apartment was even in his building.

Once in the bathroom, Treyana turned the water on in the tub, and grabbed the wet washcloth that hung on the edge of it. Reaching between her legs, she kept both feet outside of the tub, as she wiped everything on her body under the towel she was wearing, leaving her pussy and underarms completely out.

"Uh excuse me," Yvonna said as she couldn't believe her eyes. "Is that what you do every time you wash up?"

"Yeah why?"

"No wonder you're not clean."

"What do you mean?" she asked plopping on the edge of the tub.

Yvonna rolled her eyes.

"Meaning, the water has to run over you, sweetheart. You're washing up like you're gonna make a quick run. You have to *sub-*

merge that ass in the water to be considered clean. And look at the washcloth! You can't clean your body wit' that dirty ass rag!"

"Well before I couldn't get in because the tub had black stuff around it. So me and the kids washed up like this," she continued turning off the water to hear Yvonna clearly.

Yvonna was disgusted. She knew exactly what black stuff she was talking about. The cleaning crew was so sickened by the years of soap scum, dirt and grime inside of it, that they almost threw the money back at Yvonna and ran out. She had to reach a little deeper in her pockets to convince them to finish the work. Her whole plan consisted of Avante having somewhere comfortable to stay. She knew if he popped up over her house before the changes, he'd be glad he left her. In other words, Treyana's place had to compete with Cream's if her plan was going to work. She figured there had to have been something to get him to marry her in the first place. And she had to find it again.

"The tub is clean now," Yvonna said shaking her head. "Now what you have to do is run the water, get in the tub, and wash up."

"That's what I was doing," she argued hating how Yvonna was talking to her as if she was a child.

"Move out the way," she said pushing her to the side.

Yvonna ran the tub's water, then walked to the linen closet and grabbed one of the fresh clean washcloths. When the tub was full, she told her to get in.

"And lose the towel."

Covering her body, she placed herself in the water, and pulled her knees toward her breasts. For a second she could smell a fishy odor move past her nose. Smelling another woman's pussy was not something she was prepared to do so she was trying her best to save face.

"The first thing you gotta do is this," Yvonna instructed grabbing the fresh washcloth and placing it under the water. "You have to take the soap, and place it in the middle of your *wet* washcloth. Once you do that, you have to move it quickly together to form lather." Treyana remained silent. Yvonna looked at her face for understanding. "Once you have good enough lather, you start with your-,"

"Face?" Treyana let out like a six year old girl instead of a 30 year old woman.

"No," Yvonna said shaking her head. "You use a separate washcloth for your face. Never put the same washcloth on your face that you put on your ass. Understand?"

"Why not?!" she shot back feeling stupid. "It's mine!"

"Yes it is yours," Yvonna advised. "And if you want shit and piss on your face, continue to wash it like you have been but don't be surprised if you can't get a man in your bed."

"Oh I can get a man," Treyana boasted.

"No, sweetheart," Yvonna said. "I'm not talkin' about these stupid niggas you fuck wit' 'round here who lookin' for shelter from the rain. I'm talking about a real man. One like Cream got with a real job and benefits."

Silence.

"Now, you do your arms, legs and back first. I'm gonna leave out, and when you finish, call me."

"Aight," she said taking the washcloth from her.

When she was done she called Yvonna and she returned.

"Next, do your underarms," she instructed. "Now listen, your underarms need a lot of work. So you have to build up a thick enough lather to wash them thoroughly."

Treyana nodded and Yvonna left the bathroom again. When she returned, she continued with her lesson.

"Now," Yvonna smiled feeling she was finally making progress. "The main points are your pussy and ass. Always, and I do mean always, wash your pussy before you do your ass. Now here is where it gets deep," she paused. "You have to wash it very good but you also *have* to pull back the little hood, and clean around that mothafucka too. If you don't, you might as well not even be washing up."

"What hood?"

"Have you ever looked at yourself before, Treyana?"

"Not really," she laughed. "That's kinda dumb."

"No it isn't," Yvonna said looking at her like she was a science project. "You should be looking at yourself all the time. You're the first person to know if something's wrong with your body. Cuz trust and believe, them dudes you fuckin' won't care. Anyway, weren't you the same person that told me it's *yours*?" she asked growing irritated.

"Yes."

"Your hood is where you piss from. Pull the skin back, and really get in there because it holds a lot of dirt. After that, rinse your washcloth fully, and wash your ass. Got it?"

"Yeah."

"And when you're done with that," she continued placing a clean wash cloth on the tub. "Use this for your face."

Yvonna left her in the bathroom and sat in the living room on the couch. She had no idea that helping Treyana complete *her* plan would be so much work. From dropping money on the new furniture in her apartment to the new clothes in Treyana's closet, trying to get her to become presentable and sexy was a lot to do. Still if anybody could pull it off, she could.

"I'm done," she said walking into the living room with a smile on her face. "You happy now?"

"Treyana, you're the one who should be happy considering in a couple of months, you *will* be getting your husband back. Now, I've laid out the outfit I want you to wear tonight. It's on the bed. Also remember to put your makeup on like I showed you, *after* you put your clothes on. The concealer first, the foundation second and the blush and eye shadow last. If you forget anything, hit me up on my Blackberry. You got it?"

She nodded yes.

"I can't believe this is actually workin'. He ain't ever…I mean he has never called me the amount of times he has lately," she continued working on her speech. Yvonna told her that only hood rats used a lot of slang, something she had learned from the good doctor. *Although*, Yvonna did reserve the right to cuss a bitch out if need be.

"That's because he sees you're not tripping off of him anymore. All you had to do was cut him off for two weeks straight, which you have, and he'd lose his mind. But wait until he sees you tonight."

"I know!" she said jumping up and down. "He tries to say he be calling to check on the kids but whenever I answer the phone, he want to know where the fuck I've been. I can't wait to see the look on his face when I come through the doors with a man. Is he handsome for real?" she asked referring to Caven.

"Trust me, he'll make you look like a million bucks," she smiled grabbing her purse and moving toward the door. "Now he'll be here at exactly nine o'clock to pick you up. I suggest you get to know him since he'll be acting as your man for the night. When you come to the table, say only what I've told you to say and nothing else. You got it?"

"Yep."

"Aight," Yvonna smiled feeling her prodigy just might get the job done after all. "I'll see you in a little while. I told Caven to give you some money and make sure you use it on our plan."

"Don't worry! I won't let you down."

"That's good to know," she smiled reaching for the door. "Cuz it looks like *I'll*...I mean *you'll* get what you want after all."

Chapter Eighteen

No Sitter Available

"*What am I gonna do?*" Sabrina asked Yvonna as they both sat in her living room waiting on a sitter who would never come. Yvonna paid her babysitter triple to ignore Sabrina's calls.

"Maybe you won't be able to go," Yvonna said sadly. "Damn, and Cream's gonna be so hurt."

"I know!" she whined. "She needs me! I can't miss this! It's her engagement party."

"I know, but what are you gonna do? Unless…" Yvonna said looking away.

"Unless what?"

"Naw…you probably won't be up for anything like that."

"What! What! I'll do almost anything," Sabrina jumped up in her royal blue strapless dress. Her cottage cheese arms wiggling profusely.

"Well, you could leave him in the house by himself," Yvonna replied. "It ain't like he's a baby no more."

"Are you serious?" Sabrina laughed like that wasn't even an option.

"Yes I am," Yvonna said sipping the merlot in her glass. "Your son is old enough to sleep through the night. You might as well leave him by himself instead of taking him out of his own bed. That's what I would do anyway." She lied.

"I can't do that," Sabrina said as she walked around the living room. "What if he gets up in the middle of the night and comes looking for me? He'll be so scared."

"Question." Yvonna stated as she approached Sabrina in her black Emilio Pucci designer dress. "How many times has he ever gotten up in the middle of the night before?"

"Never."

"So why would he do it now, Sabrina?"

Silence.

"Listen," she smiled as she attempted to put her arm around her. When she saw it was no haps, she stopped trying. "I've been living here for the past few weeks and I see how good of a mother you are. I've also seen his patterns. And I feel comfortable in saying that your son will not get up in the middle of the night and walk out of that door. Trust me, he'll be fine."

"You think so?"

"Yes," she said tapping her on the arm. "My mother did it to me and I know Mrs. Beddows has done it to you."

They both laughed realizing everything she said was true.

"We're only going to be gone a few hours right?" Sabrina asked already at the door.

"We'll be back before he knows it," Yvonna coaxed.

They were out the door and in the car before Sabrina could change her mind. Sabrina had turned the ignition on, and was preparing to pull out when Yvonna said she forgot something.

"I'm on my period girl," Yvonna said shaking her head. "I've got to put some tampons in my purse."

"Oh…," Sabrina said. "I have some in the medicine cabinet."

"Thanks girl," Yvonna smiled. "I'll be right back."

Sabrina handed her the keys. Yvonna rushed out the car door to add the finishing touches to her maniacal plan and it took everything in her power not to laugh.

Chapter Nineteen

Snake Amongst Us

The Martini Lounge in D.C. was filled with the friends and family members of Cream and Avante. Yvonna went all out to add the finishing touches on the night. The engagement party was introduced as a gift to Cream to blind her for what Yvonna *really* had in store for her. Everybody laughed and made toasts while the snake amongst waited to attack.

"This is beautiful, Yvonna!" Cream said hugging her tightly. "I can't believe you spent all of this money on us."

"Since we're friends again, I wanted you to know how much I love you."

"Awww," she grinned taking her seat.

"What ya'll passing out hugs for?" Avante asked sitting at the table. Wearing a smoke colored suit with a black shirt, he looked handsome and sophisticated.

"I'm hugging her because of tonight. She went all out didn't she? It must be nice marrying into money."

"I can't complain," she boasted.

"They're bringing the dessert in a few minutes," Sabrina advised plopping down at the table as if it were late-breaking news.

"That's good," Yvonna was disgusted at her greed.

"So who watched Bilal Jr.?" Cream asked sipping from her Champagne.

"A sitter," Sabrina looked at Yvonna. For a second she felt ashamed leaving her son at home alone.

"Anyway," Yvonna responded trying to take the subject off of

Sabrina. "How do you like the food, Cream?"

"It's wonderful! I told you I'm feelin' everything!"

"What about you, Avante?" Yvonna asked looking toward him.

"It's on point," he winked. "You really did your thing, Ma."

Yvonna was basking in her compliments waiting for the moment when Treyana would come in and ruin it all. But instead, she saw Dave walking in with a very attractive woman on his arm. Her golden streaked hair and curvaceous body flowed as she moved toward the table.

"What up?!" Dave asked giving Avante a pound before hugging Cream and then Sabrina. He was about to hug Yvonna too, but she pulled away and extended her hand.

"What up?" Yvonna asked arm still out.

"Nothin'," he smiled catching onto the reason she was mad. Still, he shook her hand. "This is Armani Jones."

"Hi, Armani!" everyone said except Yvonna.

"I thought you weren't gonna make it man," Avante responded making room at the table for Dave and his guest.

"You know I wouldn't miss this. I can't believe ya'll about to make this thing official," he responded as Armani, connected her arm around his.

"Yeah, we're tired of playing house," he said pulling Cream closer. "I'm ready to make this woman my wife. For the rest of my life."

Cream loving the sound of his statement, nudged Yvonna underneath the table. And instead of Yvonna playing it off like she was happy for her, she kept her jealous eyes fixed onto Dave's beautiful date.

"So, Armani," Yvonna said sipping her drink. "Where do you know Dave from?" Her jealousy was consuming her and messing up her flow.

"I work with him at the community center he runs in D.C." she smiled kissing him on the cheek. "He's the bomb with kids."

"That's interesting," Yvonna smiled looking at Dave. "You don't have a problem messing with your boss? I mean, isn't that like unprofessional?"

Everybody almost gagged.

"I don't consider dealing with Dave messing with my boss because although Dave runs the center, I'm a volunteer."

"Ummmph…," Yvonna growled. "I still think it's unprofessional. I have too much respect for myself to get down like that." She totally forgot she shacked up with the good doctor while still working for him.

"Hey..hey…hey," Avante said. "This is supposed to be a special night. Let's enjoy it."

"I'm okay, Avante," Armani interrupted. "But I am concerned about her. Are you okay sweetheart?" Armani continued detecting her attitude toward her.

"I'm fine," Yvonna smiled realizing now that her reasons for coming at Armani were obvious. "Anyway," she said brushing her off. "Like Avante said, this night is supposed to be about friends. So let's celebrate!"

With that she raised her glass in the air as the others followed.

"To good times, good friends, and a long lasting marriage for Avante and Cream. May the both of you live in peace and harmony, for the rest of your lives."

Avante wrapped his arm around Cream and placed a kiss so passionate on her lips, that Yvonna got aroused.

"Excuse me," interrupted a well dressed man in a suit. "I'm, Victor Mansini the manager here, and the young lady over there has requested that I bring three bottles of Cristal to your table. Do you accept?"

When they turned around, they saw Caven with his arms wrapped around Treyana's waist as she leaned up against his chest. When Caven and Treyana saw them looking, they raised their drinks in the air and said, "Congratulations".

"Are you okay with this?" Avante asked a shocked Cream.

"Uh…sure," she said as she looked at her friends and then back at her fiancé. "I wonder what has gotten into her."

With that Mr. Mansini placed three bottles of champagne on the table that chilled on ice.

As Yvonna kept her eyes glued onto Avante, she could tell he was wondering how Treyana managed to land somebody as well off as Caven appeared. His eyes roamed to Treyana's feet and then her head. She looked like a black Barbie doll and everything about her was beautiful tonight. She was killing the "Come Fuck Me" red dress by Roberto Cavalli. His once smitten looked had been replaced with confusion and jealousy.

On queue, and just as planned, Treyana walked over to them with Caven on her arm. They looked great together and Yvonna couldn't help but smile at how well her plan was coming together.

"I hope you'll enjoy the champagne," Treyana smiled while Caven held on to her hand as if she was his lifeline.

"Yeah…thanks," Avante said. His face wore a fucked up expression. "We appreciate it."

"No problem!" she smiled again this time looking at Cream. "I just wanted to tell you that I am truly sorry for how I reacted a few weeks back. I was so caught up in my own rage and jealousy that I acted like a complete idiot. I hope you can forgive me, Cream."

The entire table was stunned. Instead of Treyana wrapping her hands around her throat, she was wrapping her up with apologies.

"Thank you, Treyana," Cream replied still holding on to the one thing she knew she wanted, Avante. "It takes a big woman to admit her wrongs."

"I know," she smiled again. Yvonna saw a brief moment of rage flow over Treyana but it went away. She was back into character. "And if you want to see your kids, you're more than welcome Avante," she responded looking at him. "I probably won't be home if you come at night, but Caven will be happy to let you in. I've enrolled in some classes at UDC, and have been tied down a lot lately."

Everyone at the table gasped. Treyana was so good that Yvonna had forgotten that she was spitting the script she'd created.

"Sure. What about tomorrow?" he asked as he frowned at the idea of another man watching his kids, and or sharing his ex-wife's bed. He liked it better when he was the best thing that ever happened to her. With all the cheating he did, he never once stopped to think that somebody out there could possibly want Treyana. After all, she was too nasty.

"Tomorrow sounds perfect!" Treyana confirmed clapping her hands together. "Well, I've taken up too much of your time already, enjoy the champagne, and your new lives together."

With that she floated away and out of the picture, leaving all of them to their thoughts.

"*Okayyyyy*," Sabrina said breaking the silence. "That was different."

"Yeah, she looks great doesn't she?" Yvonna bragged.

"I'm still trippin' out," Dave said. "Shawty, made a come back after two weeks. What the fuck happened?!"

Yvonna rolled her eyes at him, still hating on his date.

"I'm not surprised," Avante advised. "I always knew she had it in her. That's why we were together so long. But she started letting herself go."

Cream was a little envious of the comment he made about Treyana, but she let it slide.

"Well," Yvonna advised nibbling on a piece of the bread from their table. "It looks like she finally got it. Whoever her man is ain't bad either," she continued. "Anyway Sabrina, why don't you take Cream to the bathroom to fix her makeup? It looks slightly out of place."

"Oh Gawd!" Cream replied holding her face as if it would fall off. "Does it look that bad?"

"It doesn't look *bad*," Yvonna stated placing Cream's hair behind her right ear. "But you're going to be a bride soon and you should always look your best. You heard what Avante said. Don't be like Treyana and start letting yourself go."

"I wasn't talking about her Yvonna," Avante advised.

"I know. But this is her night and she's supposed to look perfect."

With that Sabrina took her away from the table, and toward the bathroom.

"Aren't you two going to dance?" she asked directing her attention to Dave and Armani.

"Naw...I don't dance," Dave informed, sipping on the champagne in his glass. He had been eye fucking Yvonna all night. "We straight ova here."

"That's no fun," Yvonna laughed. "Are you sure you're not ashamed of her?"

"Now why would I be ashamed?"

"I don't know," she said shrugging her shoulders. "You tell me."

"Let's go, Armani," he said whisking her away.

Once she had gotten rid of everyone, she moved closer to Avante.

"Can I talk to you for a moment in private?" she asked as *The Good Life* by Kanye West blasted in the background.

"Sure," he laughed. "After the way you got rid of everybody except me, I figured something was up."

"You found me out," she giggled. "What I want to talk to you about actually has to do with Cream."

"What about her?"

"Well...she shared with me something awhile back that I'd like to talk to you about...if you don't mind."

"Did she share it with you in private?"

"Kinda."

"Well why would share it with me then?"

Yvonna didn't count on his response so she didn't have an answer prepared for him. I mean, why would a man who cheated on his wife have any morals?

"*Well*...I think if I do share it with you, it could possibly be good for your marriage."

"Is that right?"

"Yes...It's like this," she said moving closer to him so that people walking by couldn't hear her. "Me and Cream had our falling out, but I miss her and want the best for her, for both of you. I know she didn't have shit to do with what happened between me and Sabrina and I treated her wrong because of it."

"Yeah," he agreed. "She took it hard when you rolled out the way you did."

"I know. That's why I'm back."

She was silent for a second to see if he'd bought any of her bullshit. But his face remained straight, and she couldn't tell if he believed her or not.

"Go ahead," he responded. "If it will bring me closer to my fiancé, it's worth hearing."

He is so fucking sickening. She thought.

"Thanks, Avante. I'd hoped you'd say that," she took a deep breath. "Cream is worried about the relationship you *don't* have with your kids."

"What about my kids?"

"Well, she thinks you could have a better one. Lately the main thing she talks to me about is having a family. Your kids are very important to her and she wants you to spend more time with them. I didn't want to say nothing, but she sorta blames you for what happened between her and Treyana the other day at the picnic."

"Why me?"

"Well she said if you were doing right by your kids, it would've never happened."

For a second he contemplated what she was saying, and when she saw he was buying it, she hammered in on him even more.

"*So*...she's been distancing herself lately because she's not sure of how to approach you about it. And with you guys getting married next month, she's scared you'll do the same thing to her. I'm not sure if she even wants to get married now." She took it too far.

"What?"

"That's why I'm talking to you. To save your engagement."

Her lies were coming together like the pieces in a puzzle. With Cream believing Avante needed space due to feeling trapped, courtesy of what she told her, and Avante thinking she wanted him to spend more time with his kids, she was ecstatic at her progress.

"Damn! She actually said that?"

"Yes."

"I had no idea she was worried about that. I mean, I want a relationship with my kids but Treyana was trippin', so I saw them when I could," he said as he looked at Cream and Sabrina exiting the restroom. "I have to talk to her," he continued as he got up to meet her.

"No!" she yelled grabbing his arm. "We weren't supposed to have this conversation remember?"

"Oh…," he said settling down. "Right."

He looked as if he didn't care to keep her secret. All he wanted to do was tell Cream that she could talk to him about anything.

"If you say anything to her about what we talked about," she continued seeing the look of desperation in his eyes. "I'm afraid it will cause tension between us again. So please don't do that. Just take my advice and see your children more. And mark my words, she'll change her behavior."

"You sure?"

"I'm positive. Trust me. Be happy she's as family oriented as she is. Imagine how she'll be when you two have kids."

"You're right," he smiled slightly.

When they returned to the table, Cream slid next to her fiancé and kissed him gently on the lips.

"What were you two talking about?" she asked as she smiled at Yvonna too.

"Us," he responded. "And the fact that I want to spend the rest of my life with you."

"And I do too." Cream responded blushing at his comment.

"You aight?" Dave asked Yvonna upon approaching the table with his date who was sweating profusely due to dancing so hard. He noticed Yvonna staring off into space like she was frightened.

Yvonna didn't move. She couldn't even speak. Because there in the doorway stood Mrs. Santana, and her eyes were glued firmly onto Caven.

Chapter Twenty

Now What?

"*Mrs. Santana!" Cream yelled hugging a* stunned woman. "You made it!!!"

"Uh…yes. I did," she said as she looked around Cream to be sure she was seeing who she saw. Caven dancing on the floor with Treyana. "I…decided to come out after all."

"Hey!" Sabrina yelled walking toward her grabbing her hand. "We're over there."

When she pointed to the table, Bernice's mouth dropped when she saw Yvonna. Yvonna was shocked also because she went over the guest-list a thousand times with Cream to be sure Bernice wouldn't show up, and each time Cream said no. If Yvonna knew she was coming she would've still showed, just with a different man for Treyana. Cream said Bernice was frazzled about something and wasn't accepting calls. But Yvonna knew who got her upset, and she was looking at him on the dance floor.

"Yvonna?" Mrs. Santana said as she looked at her evilly. "What are you doing here?"

"I'm here to support…Cr…Cream." She stuttered. "And Avante."

"I see," she smirked. "I didn't even know you were back in town," Bernice said looking for the man who caused her so much heartache recently. Ever since he came to her house and told her Bilal was gay, she hadn't eaten a thing. And she hadn't told a soul about their conversation. She was too embarrassed.

"Are you okay?" Yvonna asked knowing exactly who she was looking for.

"I think," she said placing the gift box on the table next to the others. "I can't stay long, Cream," she said managing a smile. "I just came by to show my support."

"Thanks, Ma," Avante said placing a kiss on her face. They had grown closer also. Since Yvonna had been gone, they'd formed a tight knit family. "We're glad you could make it. Even if it is for a little while."

"No problem...I figured I'd come out for a minute at least," she smiled hugging Avante back. "So, Yvonna, what brings you to town?" Her eyes pierced through her.

"Cream."

"Oh really?" she doubted taking her seat. "I didn't know you kept in touch with anyone anymore. Considering the exit you made after the accident."

"We *didn't* keep in touch," Yvonna smiled holding her head high. "But I decided to burry old hatchets."

"Is that right? Into who?"

"Excuse me?" Yvonna said leaning forward.

"Nothing," Bernice recanted. "So are you burying old hatchets for everyone?" she questioned as the entire table remained silent and observed them going back and forth.

"If you're asking me if I've forgiven your part in everything, my answer to you is yes."

"I guess I should be happy," she smiled trying to act as if their conversation wasn't out of place for the evening. "But to be honest, I don't understand what *I* did wrong. I certainly could not deny my grandson and it was *my* child who was murdered by that so-called father of yours."

"Mrs. Santana!" Cream yelled out. "Please don't do this tonight. Yvonna went through a lot of trouble for us."

"It's okay," Yvonna advised. "It sounds like she has a lot to get off her chest."

"You're right... I do. And where *is* that father of yours? The police were never able to find him after the murder of my son. Have you seen him? Or is he hiding out of town with you?"

She had seen him but she didn't have any intentions of telling

her. And even if she wanted to, she didn't know where he was staying because she got rid of him the moment he showed up at
Treyana's.

"Well nobody has attempted to get in contact with me, Bernice.
But if they do," she smiled. "I'll be more than happy to give them
any information I can. Unfortunately I haven't seen my father
since the night of the murder."

"Is that so?" Her tone condescending.

"Yes it is."

"So where are you staying?" She continued.

"Why?"

"Just asking," she smiled. "I mean, you were my son's girlfriend at one point. I'd like to make sure you're okay."

"You didn't seem to care the night you held Sabrina's baby in
your hands."

Everyone gasped.

"I mean..." she said looking around. "I'm fine and that's all
you need to know."

Now the tension at the table was beyond thick.

"Fair enough," she said, her words not matching her statement.
"So, Sabrina, where's my grandbaby?"

Yvonna heard the question but saw Caven looking over at the
table. He quickly ditched Treyana when he saw Bernice sitting
with them. Luckily they were far enough from everyone else so
Bernice couldn't see him. He rushed out the door seconds later and
Yvonna could finally relax.

"Uhh...uh...he's," Sabrina was stuttering bringing Yvonna
back to life. "He's at home."

"Who's watching him?"

It was then that Yvonna realized that she hadn't completed her
plan.

"Excuse me for a moment," she said. "I have to care for something right quick. Oh and Bernice, be careful out there." She
threatened.

"You be careful too," Bernice retaliated.

Yvonna left the table in an extreme hurry. Once outside, she grabbed an old Nokia cell phone that wasn't activated from her purse and dialed 911. She used the inactive phone instead of her Blackberry because she knew the signal wasn't traceable back to her.

"911, what's your emergency?"

"Yes…I'm calling to report a child in the street."

"What's the location?"

"2814 Prescott Drive, Hyattsville, MD."

"Okay, mam, did you remove the child from the street?"

"He left before I could get a hold of him," she lied. "But I think he walked back into the house. I'm not sure. He was almost hit by a car."

"How old did the child look?"

Yvonna wanted to cuss the operator out for asking a million questions. *Just go get the mothafucka!* She thought.

"Yvonna?" Dave said walking behind her.

Without waiting, she disconnected from the operator and turned around to face him. She only hoped the police would follow her lead and go to the house to find the child home alone. Because once they arrived, they'd find the door propped wide open, courtesy of her.

"What do you want, boy?" she wondered if he'd heard her call.

"I was just makin' sure you was aight. Why you always got an attitude wit' me?"

"Because I hate you, didn't you know?"

"Naw…all I can remember was the way you were staring me down at the table."

"I was not!" she lied. "Anyway, shouldn't you be tending to your little girlfriend?" She asked throwing the cell phone in her purse.

"She aight."

"I'm sure," she said trying to conceal her jealousy.

"I just wanted you to know I wasn't feelin' Mrs. "S" and how she treated you in there."

"Whatever," she said waving him off as she searched her purse for a piece of gum. Ever since she'd given up smoking, she turned to gum. "You should've told her back there."

"I did."

He shut her down quick.

"Why are you always so concerned about me Dave? Stop sweatin!"

"You wish I was sweatin' ya ass," he was about to walk away but saw her rummaging through her purse. Something about her attitude appealed to him. "Need a light?"

"No...I quit," she responded locating her gum. Now if you can get out of my face, I'll be fine. I just needed some air from all the fakeness."

Instead of walking away from her, he grabbed both of her shoulders and kissed her firmly on the lips. The longer he held her, the more she melted. His scent, his strength and his forwardness were all turn on's. *The nerve.* She thought never removing away from him.

"I see you ain't talkin' shit now," he said finally letting her go. Her lips still puckered.

With that he walked off, leaving her standing in her own lust.

When he left, she looked around to see if anyone saw how he played her. She was alone. But Yvonna realized then that the game would be played differently. And if she didn't pull herself together, she would lose.

Chapter Twenty-One

Another One Down

"*I'm gonna need you to calm down* mam," the officer advised as he stood over Sabrina. She was screaming and begging them to let her speak, and each time she opened her mouth, nothing audible came out.

"Pl..ple..ase let me ex…ex..plain," she sobbed. "I was only gone for two hours."

"Mam," the male officer started while the female officer remained silent in the background. "You can't leave a child this young home for five minutes by himself, let alone two hours!" Bilal Jr. played on the floor with his toy truck, totally unaware of what was going on around him.

"But I'm sooooorry," she cried as Yvonna sat on the left of her pretending to be on her side.

"Officer," Yvonna said looking up at him with kind eyes. "Can I talk to you alone please?"

"I don't know what's left to say," he advised placing the pen in his shirt pocket. "Once Child Protective Services arrives, we are taking him to a more stable environment. And that really *is* the bottom line."

"Please," she pleaded. "Just five minutes. I believe I can shed some light on this situation."

"Alright," he said reluctantly. "Five minutes over by the kitchen. And make it quick." Yvonna hugged Sabrina tightly and promised to be right back.

"Let me go talk to him," she whispered. "Maybe he'll listen to me."

"Thank you," Sabrina mumbled, as if she'd already won the serious cop over. When they were alone in the kitchen the cop got right to the point.

"What's up?" he asked his brow creasing with disgust.

"I wanted to tell you that I'm happy you're taking him away from her," she started.

"Come again," he leaned in.

"I said I'm with you," she whispered peaking her head out, only to see Sabrina staring in their direction. Walking further in the kitchen to hide her lips from Sabrina's sight she continued. "She has left him home alone on more than one occasion. When she goes to work…when she wants to go out and everything else. And I can't count the number of times he's starved. I live in Baltimore sir, and I came all the way out here because I was worried about my Godson. You have to help him."

"Well why did you allow her to leave him here tonight? If you're so worried."

"She lied to me," she looked down at his steel toe boots to get his glaze off her lying eyes. "She told me she had a sitter for him. When I came home to find your car outside, I was just as shocked as you were."

He cleared his throat and looked into her eyes. Yvonna tried her best to keep a straight and concerned expression on her face. Both were difficult because she was elated that things were working out her way.

"How long has this been going on?"

"Ever since she first had him," she advised keeping her voice down. "After all this time, she finally got caught. I can't stand by and watch this happen anymore."

"Thanks Mam," he responded placing his hand on her left shoulder. "I know it was hard to see the cute little guy be treated this way. But I'm happy you were brave enough to step up."

Sabrina caught a glimpse of his and Yvonna's smile, and was hopeful that maybe she was able to talk some sense into the serious cop.

With that they walked back in the living room, and Yvonna disappeared into the bedroom before returning. The officer kept his eyes on Sabrina, and frowned even more due to what Yvonna told her. The only thing that stopped him from giving her an additional piece of his mind was his walkie-talkie going off and her son playing on the floor.

"We're here now. Please have the child ready."

"Roger that." He responded into his radio. "You got any clothes you want to give us to take with your son?"

"Nooooooo!" she screamed dropping to the officer's feet. And as if she was the plague, he backed away and demanded that she pull herself together. "Please don't take my son! Please! Oh my God he's all I got."

She scared Lil Bilal and he instantly began to cry.

"You should've thought about that before you neglected him," he smiled. "I'm just happy you have people like this young lady right here around, who care enough to tell the truth. Who knows where he might've ended up."

The female officer lifted Bilal Jr. off the floor, as he screamed for his mother with outstretched arms.

Running up to the baby, Sabrina bombarded him with kisses almost knocking the officer and the child to the floor. The male officer had to pull her body off of theirs, to free them from her weight and strength.

When plain clothes officers arrived, they took the child away as Sabrina continued to beg them to reconsider.

"Sorry Mam," a white lady with stringy blonde hair said. "But we need to evaluate the situation in full before returning the child to your custody. Someone will be in contact."

When the door was closed, Sabrina fell to her knees rocking everything within a few feet. One of the pictures frames on the table fell to the floor and shattered into little pieces. Yvonna bent down and helped her up, hugging her tightly.

"Its gonna be okay honey," she said wrapping her arms around her, as best she could. "You'll see."

She sounded sympathetic and even proceeded in wiping Sabrina's tears with her bare hands. And just like she promised years ago, she wiped her ass with them. Sabrina was too distraught to notice.

"But what am I gonna do without my son Yvonna? I can't live without him!" She sobbed.

Yvonna frowned at her. She must've seriously thought she gave a fuck.

"I remember that feeling," Yvonna said as if she was another person. "I felt the same way years ago. You remember…when I found out about Bilal and you. But you know what, I got over it, and you will too."

"What?" she said wiping her tears. She wasn't sure she heard Yvonna correctly.

"I said," she smiled looking devious. "I got over losing someone I loved too. And I got over the fact that you laid your fat funky ass down with my man, and you're gonna have to get used to losing your child. Isn't that funny," she chuckled. "We both lost Bilal. Mine in death, and yours with child protective services."

Sabrina stood looking at her with widened eyes.

"Umm...Umm…Umm…," she said shaking her head. "It's hard to believe that he laid on top of you, let alone fucked you. But revenge is soooo sweet. Isn't it?"

"Are you telling me you had something to do with what happened to my son?" Sabrina asked looking at her with hate.

"*Something* to do with it?" she laughed. "I had *everything* to do with this shit! I told you I'd get you back for what you did to me, and this is it. I couldn't stand that lil mothafucka anyway! He was bad as shit."

Sabrina went to hit her and Yvonna whipped out a pocket knife. She dared her to step.

"Bitch I wish you would!"

"Get out of my, house!" She screamed. "Now!"

"Don't worry honey," she laughed. "I'm already one up on you," she continued lifting the Louis Vuitton suitcases she had in the living room. She went to grab them right after talking to the officer but Sabrina didn't notice. "And don't bother telling Cream about this little mishap. Just stay out of my way, and let her receive what she has coming to her. Because if I find out that you so much as whispered what happened tonight to Cream, you'll find out that the separation from your son will be more than temporary. It will be permanent. Because I'll hound child protective services daily to tell them how bad of a mother you are."

With that she walked out the door, got in the truck, and crossed Sabrina's name off the list.

Chapter Twenty-Two

Moving Closer

"*She still not answering her phone, Yvonna,*" Cream said as she sat in the 2007 cherry red Lexus 350 Yvonna rented. Throwing her phone in her purse, she looked out the car window, and then back at Yvonna.

"Why are you so worried about her answering the phone anyway?" she asked as she reached forward and tucked Cream's hair behind her ear. "Your weddings in one week and you should be focusing on that." Yvonna pulled out her Blackberry awaiting an urgent text message. "Stop worrying about Sabrina's jealous ass!"

"But she's one of my bridesmaids," Cream whined. "And it's like she's fallen off the face of the earth," She continued as tears formed in her eyes. "First the loan fell through for the house, and now Sabrina! What is going on lately?"

This bitch is a crybaby if I've ever saw one!

"I'm sorry about the house Cream," She said not wanting to hang on that topic too long. "But Sabrina is not to be trusted," she turned around to face her with the Blackberry still in hand. "You saw what she did to me with Bilal. She probably wants to fuck Avante too for all we know."

"Don't say that," she said holding her mouth.

"It's true! You better watch that bitch. And now that I'm back in your life, I'll make sure it won't happen to you."

"I know," she smiled. "But I still don't get it. We were so close and all of a sudden she's ignoring me like I did something wrong to her. I wonder if she's mad that I made you my maid of honor."

"Could be," Yvonna said shrugging her shoulders.

When Yvonna saw "1 New Message" appear across her Blackberry, she un-knowingly blurted out, "About time!"

"What's that?" Cream asked.

"Oh…I've been waiting to hear something from my business associate and he's finally contacted me. Anyway," she responded diverting the conversation elsewhere. "What's going on with you and Avante?"

"He's been tripping lately," Cream said looking out the window again. "To be honest Yvonna, I'm not sure if we're going to be married now."

"Don't say that. You two deserve each other."

"It's the truth. I think he's cheating on me."

"Now why would he do that?" Yvonna questioned, already knowing the answer.

"I don't know I just do. Let's not forget how we got together. He did leave and divorce his wife because of me."

"He did that because ya'll were supposed to be together that's why! That's not your fault you guys fell in love."   "You think?"

"Yes!" she said hitting her leg. "Don't get stage fright now. After all this money I spent on your ass."

Both women laughed.

"So why has he been hanging over Treyana's house every other day then?"

"He's been what?" Yvonna acted like she didn't know.

"Everyday he's been over Treyana's house. When I ask him what the deal is, he claims he's spending more time with his kids."

"Damn…everyday huh?"

"Yeah…are you thinking what I'm thinking?"

Yvonna was silent for a second. Inside she was laughing so hard it almost showed.

"Kinda…I mean, if he's doing this all of a sudden maybe he's….naw," Yvonna said as if she'd changed her mind. "He ain't fucking with Treyana. She's a mess."

"She *was* a mess remember?" Cream advised referring to the night she looked like a black Barbie doll.

"Oh…right. How long has this been again?"

"Ever since we saw her at the club a few weeks ago."

"I don't know," Yvonna said taking her keys from the ignition. "Let's just hope for the best. And in the mean time, we're going to go into that mall and spend some more of my money."

"I'm wit' that!" Cream said exiting the car.

When they walked through Prince Georges Plaza, they stopped by Auntie Anne's Pretzels to grab some snacks as Yvonna's eyes scanned the mall.

"Are you looking for somebody?"

"I'm not looking for nobody girl," she lied.

And suddenly Yvonna's face produced a huge grin. When Cream looked in the direction Yvonna was looking in, her heart broke when she saw Avante and Treyana laughing and joking in the mall with the twins between them.

"Avante," Cream said approaching them, the smiles were wiped from their faces.

"Oh…uh…hey, baby," Avante said. "Me and Tree were just taking the kids shopping."

"Tree?" she said repeating the pet name he'd given her. She was usually called dirty bitch, whore and loud mouth.

"I mean, Treyana," he corrected himself clearing his throat first.

"I see." She was so upset at Avante, that she didn't see Yvonna and Treyana trading smirks.

"What are you two doing here?" Avante asked looking at her and Yvonna.

"Yvonna wanted to take me to buy something to wear for my bachelorette party."

"Is that right?" he asked believing there was more to the story than Cream knew.

"Yes, well, I'll leave you two alone. Come on Yvonna," Cream continued grabbing her hand in a hurry. She had to get away from the scene.

"Talk to ya'll later," Yvonna smiled walking off with Cream. Avante and Treyana remained a few seconds before walking away.

"Bye Cream." Treyana called out before she winked. Avante

didn't see her.

"That's it," Cream sobbed uncontrollably searching her purse for a tissue. "The wedding's off!"

Are you serious? Yvonna thought. She hadn't even had a chance to really destroy their relationship yet. She felt Cream was making things far too easy. It wasn't like they didn't have kids together. Don't get it twisted. She knew she would be upset after seeing them together and that's why she planned the little run in. But this was supposed to be the "set up" before the big finale.

"Maybe you *should* rethink the wedding," she advised before feeling her phone vibrate. "I didn't know how bad it really was between you two until now. Excuse me Cream."

"What is it Caven?" she whispered angrily into the phone. "I'm busy right now."

"You need to come to the hotel right away."

"For what?" she asked looking at Cream with kind eyes.

"I can't tell you over the phone."

"Either you tell me now or see me later."

"I can't," he responded. "Just get here right away."

With that he hung up. Yvonna wasn't too concerned about whatever he had to tell her. She was more worried about being able to cross Cream's name off that list of hers.

"Now what were you saying?" she asked moving toward her.

"When I asked him where he was going earlier," she said wiping her tears with a greasy Auntie Pretzel napkin. "He didn't mention anything about seeing the kids. He told me he was going over his mother's house. So why he lie Yvonna?"

Yvonna was stunned. She didn't know Avante lied to her about his whereabouts. This was even better than she imagined because she never thought he'd *actually* leave Cream who was beyond sexy for Treyana who was *alright*. But if things continued the way that they were, she'd be finished with her list by the end of the week.

Chapter Twenty-Three

New Plan Of Action

When Yvonna pulled up in front of the hotel, she noticed a familiar car. Just the sight of it sent chills through her spine because she knew the person it belonged to had it custom made. The Lamborghini doors on the Corvette with the silver streaks down the side were unique. But to be sure, she glanced at the license plate and almost stumbled. *DRTERELL.*

Maybe he's here on some Doctor's convention. She thought remembering how much he used to travel.

"Yvonna! Yvonna!" a male voice yelled from an undetermined location.

When she didn't look due to examining the car, the person became persistent. Turning toward the voice, she saw Swoopes in the passenger seat of a White Yukon Denali with a black eye patch over his left eye. She hadn't planned on seeing him and was quite aware of how he felt about her. She almost dropped her shopping bags due to being so frightened.

What the fuck is going on around here? She thought. When Dave got out of the driver seat and walked up on her, she was a little relieved they came together. She thought Swoopes was there to kill her.

"I got to talk to you!" he said frantically.

"For what? And how you know I was here?"

"Sabrina told me you weren't staying with her no more," he advised as a look of urgency came over his face. "So I asked Cream and she told me where to find you."

"Well I can't talk now," she responded as she briefly looked him up and down. He looked so much like the rapper "Young Buck" without the corn rolls that it was scary.

She turned to walk away but he grabbed her wrist. He let her go remembering the last time he held her against her will.

"Look," he said looking around to be sure no one was listening. "The police been round the way askin' questions 'bout you. Somebody said you were in town."

"What they want from me?" she questioned looking over at Swoopes who was frowning.

"Dave, come on man," Swoopes hollered. "We gotta be at the shop by 7:00! Ain't nobody got time for that bitch!"

"Fuck you!" Yvonna yelled.

"Nigga hold up," he said turning around irritated at his outburst. "Look," he turned back to Yvonna. "Call me here." He handed her a card which read, *"Dave Walters, Each One Teach One. Children's advocate."*

"Whatever," she responded taking the card from him and tossing it in one of her bags. "I'll call you when I can. And what happened to his eye?"

"It's a long story." With that he dipped off. Her eyes met Swoope's once more before they sped off. He hated her and she felt it.

When they left she took the elevator upstairs to her room. And when she opened the door, the first thing she saw was Caven sitting on a chair, with his elbows on his knees, and his face in his hands.

Usually Caven greeted her the moment she hit the door, but this time he looked toward his left. When she pushed the door open wider, she saw Terrell sitting on the couch. The door slamming shut was all that could be heard in the room. He found her ass.

"What are you doing here?" she said trying to appear as if she had everything under control. Placing the bags up against the wall, she kicked her shoes off.

"I'm here for you?" he responded as he stood up and walked toward her.

Yvonna looked at Caven wondering what possessed him to let

Terrell into the room to begin with. She wasn't tripping though. She'd deal with his ass later.

"Don't be mad at Caven," he responded noticing how she was mugging him. "He had no choice. I have enough information on him that would ruin his life. Don't I Caven?"

Caven didn't respond.

"Well what do you want with me?" She busied herself with emptying her shopping bags doing her best not to appear nervous.

"I came for you," he responded as he sat back down. He was wearing a brown pinstriped suit with a pink shirt and tie to match. Although many men couldn't pull off the pink and brown combo, Terrell wasn't just any man. The suit itself ran five thousand dollars and Yvonna could tell.

"For me huh?" she giggled. "Well I'm not interested in trash-dick, so you can turn back around and leave out the door."

"Bitch I want my money," he continued angry at her comment. "You didn't think you could take eighty thousand from me, and I'd just accept it did you?"

"I wasn't thinking about you at all," she said as she poured herself a glass of vodka, straight up no ice. She swallowed the entire glass, felt it stream down her throat, and downed another. She decided to swallow a third after seeing him trying to read her mind. "So get the fuck out."

"Now, now, now," Terrell responded as he stood up, removed the glass from her hands, and drank its contents. "What'd I tell you about using that kind of language? It's not lady like."

She snatched the glass, poured another and threw it in his fucking face.

"And what'd I tell you about trying to change me?" She smiled as she watched the vodka pour down his face and expensive suit. "Don't!"

He calmly opened his jacket, removed a handkerchief and wiped his face and suit. Afterwards he smacked her in the face with the back of his hand. She laughed and her reaction scared him.

"Listen, bitch, you fucked with the wrong one. Don't let the degree on my wall and this smooth face fool you. I was raised in the Bronx bitch!"

Damn! Yvonna thought. *If he woulda acted like this before maybe I'da kept his ass.*

"Now I want my money," he continued as he grabbed a card from his pants. "And not a penny under eighty thou. Make no mistake, if you fuck with me, I *will* ruin your life. Or what's left of it anyway." With that he handed her his card with a number handwritten on the back. "I'm staying at the Sheraton hotel in DC. Call me when you get it. All of it," he continued as he left out the door.

Yvonna was so angry with Caven that she could've stole his weak ass in the face. But she had bigger fish to fry. The last thing she needed was Terrell and the police on her back. And she wished she had the one person who always knew what to do in a situation like this around...Gabriella.

Chapter Twenty-Four

Straight Up

Gabriella was wearing all red. She sat across the table with her legs crossed eyeing Yvonna as if she couldn't be more disgusted with her. Yvonna was just thinking about her after dealing with Terrell when she walked out to her car and saw Gabriella standing there. She was always on time.

"And you did what again?" she questioned.

"There was nothing I could do." she responded as she waited on the waitress to come and take their orders. "He found me!"

"You shouldn'tve let his ass walk out the door alive," she responded as she placed a cigarette in her mouth and lit it. Just looking at it made Yvonna want one. "All he's gonna do is cause more problems than you need. And where is this fuckin' waitress?!" she yelled looking around. "This bitch is gonna make me cuss her out!"

Just when she was coming to take their orders, Gabriella got up to use the bathroom.

"Order my food before I choke that bitch out!" she responded extra loud putting the cigarette out.

The waitress came back to the table with an attitude and she wondered if she heard Gabriella and her loud outburst.

"Can I take your orda!" the light skin rude waitress asked. She had freckles all over her face, and looked as if she hadn't combed her hair all year.

What's up with these bitches not grooming themselves?!! Yvonna thought.

"Yes," Yvonna responded throwing the same shade. "I'll take

the *Three For All* platter, and the *Friday's Shrimp* with fries please," she continued hoping the waitress would give her a reason to swell on that ass.

"And what you want to drink?!" she asked, still obviously pissed off.

"Bring a Coke and a Sprite." The waitress turned around and was about to leave before Yvonna said, "And when you come back, lose the attitude."

The girl stomped off disappearing into the kitchen.

"She got the orders," Yvonna said as thoughts of the doctor and what she was going to do entered her mind.

"She was too slow and I'ma have something to say to her ass when she get back," she promised.

"Please let me deal with her," Yvonna pleaded. "It's not that serious."

When she returned the waitress placed both drinks on Yvonna's side of the table and walked off.

"You saw that shit right?" Gabriella said. "She betta be glad I don't have time for this shit today."

Yvonna was relieved because picking a fight with the waitress was not what she had in mind.

"So what should I do?"

"You know what I think you should do," Gabriella said as she pulled her compact out of her purse and checked her makeup. "You should kill his ass."

She was about to sip her drink when she saw something thick cloudy and white floating in it.

"Hold up," Gabriella said forgetting all about the murder comment. "I think this bitch spit in my drink."

Yvonna looked inside and sure nuff it looked like spit. Hock spit at that.

"No it don't." Yvonna lied. "It looks like fizz."

"Bitch this ain't no fizz! This spit!"

Gabriella started breathing heavily. Yvonna knew exactly what was up. She was getting ready to go off with a whole rack of witnesses watching. The only thing that could convince Gabriella that it wasn't spit was Yvonna drinking it herself. So to save the girl's life, and avoid commotion, she drank from her cup.

"See?" Yvonna responded feeling the clumpy mass go down her throat. "Betta now?"

"Yeah whateva," Gabriella said snatching her drink back. "Like I said, you gonna have to take the doctor's ass out and I'm not talking about on a date."

"I can't do that," Yvonna whispered as she looked around to see if anyone overheard her. When she felt it was safe to talk she said, "I still don't know if they found out we had anything to do with killing Theodorus."

"Did you hear anything on the news about his ass?"

"No," Yvonna said.

"Cuz ain't nobody trippin'! So we got away with it. You got to remember, we live in a country that trains killers for war. Surely they won't miss one pimple-fetish-freak!"

"Yeah but that don't mean they won't notice if a doctor shows up missing." Yvonna whispered again.

"Listen," she responded slowly. "All he's gonna do is cause problems for you. He has to be eliminated. Unless you still got *all* of his money."

"Even if I did have all of it he wouldn't get it back." she continued as she sat up straight when the waitress returned with their food. "Give me a sec. Wait until she leaves."

And just like she did the last time, she placed both plates on Yvonna's side of the table.

"Bitch I had enough of your shit!" Gabriella responded. "One of them plates belong to me."

The waitress rolled he eyes at Yvonna and walked off.

"She must've heard you cuss her out earlier," Yvonna replied. "Don't even trip!"

"I got somethin' for that bitch later," she responded as she watched her walk off. "But anyway," she continued as she grabbed a potato wedge and swallowed it whole. "If you don't want to kill your precious doctor it's gonna get worse. We have to do it and you have to trust me," she responded as she grabbed a wing and downed it with some Sprite. "Have I steered you wrong yet?"

Yvonna didn't respond. She just left things in her hands.

Chapter Twenty-Five

This Bitch

"*She finally called,*" Cream yelled on the other end of the phone. "But she didn't sound too happy."

"Well what did she say?" Yvonna asked as she sat up straight in the car, upon hearing the news. If Sabrina opened her mouth she had something for that bitch already planned.

"Nothin' much," she said in a low voice. "Just that she had to talk to me later."

Yvonna's heart beat fast. "Did she say what it was about?"

"Nope, just mentioned your name and asked me if we were still cool." Yvonna was silent as she contemplated her next move. "Are ya'll okay?"

"No. I realized I can't get past her deceit. So when ya'll spose to meet?" she questioned.

"Tomorrow."

"Good!" Yvonna let out by mistake. She figured the later she hooked up with her the better. She needed to execute part two of her plan for Sabrina since it was obvious she couldn't keep her fat lips closed.

"Why you say that?"

"No reason," Yvonna responded. "It's just that we have some things to take care of for the wedding this week, and I'll be needing most of your time."

"I still don't know about the wedding," Cream said as if she was on the verge of crying.

While driving and listening to a whiney ass Cream cry about her life, she overheard on the radio that a homicide occurred at the Friday's Restaurant in P.G. County last night. A waitress was shot and killed in the parking lot and video footage existed of the suspect.

It can't be! She thought as Gabriella entered her mind. She was about to push the thought of her being involved out of her mind until they stated the victim was affectionately known as "Freckles" by her co-workers and friends. If the waitress had anything, freckles were it.

"Hold that thought," Yvonna said. "I'ma call you right back Cream."

Without waiting on her response, she pulled over on a side street in Georgetown, DC, a few blocks away from the strip on Wisconsin Avenue where the stores were located. She felt herself hyperventilating.

She pulled the visor down and looked at herself in the mirror. She was sweating and looked awful. She didn't want Dave, who she was meeting in a few minutes to see her like this. Yvonna grabbed a napkin out of the glove compartment and patted her forehead.

"Okay…," she said taking a deep breath. "Calm down. You have to pull yourself together. Everything is gonna be okay and there's no proof Gabriella was involved," she continued still talking to herself. With that she reached inside her black Prada pocketbook, and pulled out her compact to reapply the foundation and lipstick she was wearing.

It was important that she looked good because she hadn't forgotten about Dave, and crossing his name off her list. She had plans to seduce him to a point where he needed her to breathe. And the way he looked into her eyes, she was positive it would work. Yvonna didn't stop to think that she was feeling him too.

She hopped out of the rented Lexus, and brushed herself off with her hands. She was killing her Coogi jeans and the studded white sleeveless shirt that revealed her cleavage. Her hair was freshly done, and the moment her shoes hit the street, all eyes were on her.

Just as planned, she went to Phillips restaurant and took her seat. Dave wasn't there. She checked her Movado watch several times as if watching it would make him appear. *This mothafucka's getting on my nerves already.* She thought.

"May I take your order," a thin white lady asked. Her voice was soft and kind and she instantly changed Yvonna's negative mood.

"Yes, I'll take a glass of water with lemon please." The lady was turning to leave when Yvonna placed her hand on her forearm stopping her. "Oh and uh…very little ice."

"Sure!" she responded as if she was eager to serve her. "Will your guest be ordering anything?"

"I don't know," she stated glancing at her watch again. "He's already late." When the waitress left, she came back with a bottle of Merlot.

"I didn't order that," Yvonna advised thinking the young woman made a mistake.

"Oh no," she smiled. "This was purchased by Mr. Walters. He called and told us to bring you over a bottle of your favorite wine. He said he wasn't sure but he believed it was Merlot. Is he right?"

"Oh…uh…yes," she responded.

"Great! He also said to make sure you're satisfied, he'd like you to order whatever you wanted from the menu."

Yvonna had plans to do that anyway. But she couldn't help but smile at Dave's thoughtfulness. And when she began to tell herself that he wasn't half bad, she remembered that it was because of him that she lost her baby.

"Thanks," Yvonna responded. "In that case, I'll take the best steak and lobster you have to offer." When the woman was preparing to leave she touched her arm again and said. "Oh and as an appetizer I'd like some cocktail shrimp."

"Right away Mam," she nodded.

Fifteen minutes later, and right after the last shrimp was stuffed in her mouth, Dave walked in talking on his phone. To be changed like he claimed he was, he still acted like a thug. And for some reason that made her panties wet.

He came in wearing blue Seven jeans, a very expensive belt with a buckle in the shape of a skull head outlined in diamonds on the front. He also had on a white tank top and was freaking a pair of white and red retro Jordan's. He completed his look with a red Chicago Bulls cap tilted slightly toward the side. His muscular arms were out and Yvonna had to stop what she was feeling upon seeing his fine ass. When he saw her eyeing him up, he winked and smiled at her.

"Aigh't, man," he said finishing the call. "I'm out." He stuffed his phone in his pocket. "What you lookin' at, girl?"

"One late mothafucka," she responded. "Why you wear that shirt anyway? Ain't you cold?"

"Yeah whateva," he laughed. "Don't get mad at me cuz you gettin' wet over there."

She looked down quickly thinking her lust showed. When she realized that was ridiculous, she looked back up at him.

"Don't flatter yourself. And why were you late? I hate that shit."

"One of the kids at my center got locked up for pulling up street signs and rearranging them. I had to bail his bad ass out."

"Well I was just getting ready to leave," she lied. "So you betta be glad you came when you did."

"I betta be glad?" he leaned in as he repeated the statement. "You the one need to be glad. I'm lookin' out for yo ass. You done had shrimp *and* wine and shit! I hooked that ass up."

"Yeah okay, Dave!" she responded hating that she was feeling something for him. Just like she had in the car, the day of the accident, no matter how much she hated him, she couldn't deny the obvious attraction she felt toward him. "I can look out for my damn self."

"Listen at you," he smiled.

"Here's your meal, Mr. Walters," The waitress said placing his food on the table. He called ahead to be sure his food was there when he arrived. "Preciate it Ma!" he winked. And then she placed Yvonna's food in front of her.

When the waitress left, Yvonna looked at Dave wondering what his deal was. *He probably do this weak ass shit all the time.*

"Are you gonna tell me what's up?" she asked as she watched

him scarf down a whole portion of mashed potatoes in one sitting.

"Uh yeah," he started as he swallowed part of what was in his mouth. "Like I said, the cops is lookin' for dat ass."

"For what?"

"You know," he continued placing his fork down on the plate, causing it to make a clinking noise. "They haven't been able to find your father. So they heard you were in town, and started coming around asking questions again."

Yvonna figured right way it was Sabrina's hot ass who put them on to her, or Bernice.

"Well what do they want from me?" she asked as if he'd know. "I told them everything I knew about Bilal's murder. They should be looking for my father instead of wasting their time on me."

"I don't know," he continued as he downed half a glass of water. "Maybe they think you're lyin'."

"Well I can't be blamed for bad detective work. Did you talk to them?"

"No, but my mom did. She don't know nothin' though."

"So I guess they been by Sabrina's?"

"Naw," he continued as he devoured his baked chicken as if he was on lockdown fearing somebody would snatch it from his plate. "You not fuckin' wit Sabrina no more?"

"I don't want to talk about it. And why are you tellin' me? I mean, what's in it for you?"

"I don't know," he continued as he wiped his mouth with the cloth napkin. "I guess I'm lookin' out for you."

"Well I don't need charity," she said sipping from her glass. "So if it'll help, I forgive you for all that you've done," she lied. With that she stood up as she prepared herself to leave.

"Sit down," he said in a low voice.

"What?"

"I said sit down," he continued as he took the cap off his head and placed it on the table looking deeply into her eyes. He was trying to tell her something and Yvonna wished he'd say it. She was so mesmerized by how attractive he was that she obeyed his command and remained seated.

"What if I told you I wanted to see you too? What would you say then?"

"I'd say don't waste your time because you have a girlfriend. That whack ass kiss wasn't enough to make nobody trip."

"Yeah right."

"Let's just call it what it is," she said as she folded her hands on the table. "You want to taste my pussy don't you?"

"Hell yeah. Now the question is, will you let me?"

Her pussy was pulsating and she despised the control he had over her. She wanted him…more than she did anybody in a long time. In a lot of ways he reminded her of Bilal, and because of it, she hated and liked him all at once. But what was she going to do? She was feeling him too much to get revenge. She was planning to fake like she cared about him to break his heart, but now she was really falling.

"Thanks for the info," she responded grabbing her purse. "But I'm not interested."

"Yvonna, I can smell how bad you want me from all the way over here."

"Bye!" She reached in her purse and placed two hundred dollars on the table. "I trust that'll be enough for the bill. I pay my own way in life."

"Stop runnin' Yvonna."

"Bye, Dave!"

"The more you fight the more it'll happen between us," his voice raised over the chatter in the restaurant.

She didn't respond, just walked out.

She couldn't understand why everyone else was easy to conquer yet he remained the hardest. Whatever the "*Thing*" was he had over her, she knew she had to grab a hold of it. But before she could deal with him, she had to check Sabrina's ass. Then she had to finish Cream and finally she had to find out what to do about Terrell and his sudden visit. It didn't help that the cops were on her heels now either. But this was the game she chose to play.

Chapter Twenty-Six

Finishing Shit Off

Yvonna knocked vigorously at Sabrina's door. A little impatient she glanced down at the brown mat outside. It read *Welcome* in large blue letters. She wondered if she'd still feel that way after she got finish with her ass. Frankly it didn't matter if she opened the door or not because either way, she was coming in.

"Who is it?!" a tired voice yelled from behind the other side. Caven and Yvonna remained silent, hiding from view.

Instead of turning around like most sane people would after receiving a strange knock at the door in the middle of the night, Sabrina flung it open. When she did she was met with a serious blow to the face, courtesy of Caven. Caught off balance she attempted to scream but her sound was muted by Caven who had placed one hand over her mouth after knocking her to the couch. Yvonna ran through the house to be sure no one was there. She was all alone.

"Sit the fuck down and don't move!" Caven demanded. Yvonna took joy in the fright on her face.

She was dressed well for the occasion wearing an all black catsuit by Jean Paul Gaultier, black gloves, and ankle length Louis Vuitton boots with the Mimosa Monogram imprinted upon them. She even wore the extra large black shades to accentuate her "Ready For War" look.

"Hello, Sabrina," she smiled taking the glasses off revealing the smoky eye shadow she always wore. "What I tell you about gettin' in my fuckin' business?"

"What's going on, Yvonna?" Sabrina asked her voice quivering. Caven remained standing over her, with the gun placed firmly to her head. "What did I do?"

"What's going on?" she repeated sarcastically. "Bitch I warned you against speaking to Cream didn't I? And what do you do? Break our little arrangement."

"I didn't say anything to Cream!"

"You're right," she smiled. "You haven't said anything to Cream yet and that's why I'm here now. To check your ass. I know all about the little meeting you were *supposed* to have with her tomorrow. So I'm here to make good on my promise to you."

Yvonna reached into the strapless Juicy Couture bag she had nestled under her arm, and removed a syringe.

"What is that Yvonna?! What are you getting ready to do to me?" her body moved frantically on the couch. That's when Caven followed up with another blow to her face, using the butt of the gun.

"Thanks sweetheart," she winked at him. "I don't have to tell you what will happen if you talk or make another sound again now do I?" Sabrina held her face as the pain rippled through the open wound.

"Do you think you're gonna get away with this Yvonna?" she cried. "Everybody knows what's wrong with you. You need help."

"I don't need help," the smile was removed from her face. "I just like to make sure that people like you know betta than to fuck wit' me," she walked toward the couch. "Now hold out your fuckin' arm."

"No!?" she cried uncontrollably.

"C...hit this bitch again!"

On command he hit her again with the end of the gun. She screamed out and Caven was positioning himself to whack her in the mouth a second time but she ceased crying and held out her arm.

"I knew you'd see it my way," Yvonna continued as she stooped down in front of Sabrina. Grabbing her wrist she said, "It's so much easier when you comply now isn't it?"

Sabrina remained silent.

"Now this is gonna sting a little," she advised. "But I promise the feeling will go away soon enough."

"Why are you doing this me?" she sobbed as the burning sensation ran through her body. "Do I really deserve all of this?"

Yvonna's evil stare let her know how she felt about the question.

"What are you putting into me?"

"It's heroine. Roll with it baby."

"What!" she yelled snatching her arm back as the needle broke off into her skin. "Ouuuccchh," she cried out. It was too late the contents had already entered her bloodstream.

Yvonna didn't remove the broken needle. It wouldn't bother her where she was going anyway.

"Now that that's done," she continued as she retrieved a folded paper from her purse. "I need you to sign this, and then we'll leave."

"What is it?" she cried wiping her eyes trying to clear up her sudden blurred vision.

"It's just a little something. Now sign it or I'll go to where your precious little boy is and kill him too. You should know by now I'm not fuckin' wit you."

"I'm not signing anything!" Sabrina yelled.

"Do you think I'm joking? Even after all of this?"

"I hate you!" Sabrina yelled.

"Bitch sign the fuckin' letter," Yvonna replied slapping her face. "I'm not going to ask you again."

Sabrina got up enough energy to sign the letter as she felt herself suddenly unable to breath. Although she'd never taken drugs before, she was sure heroine wasn't supposed to make her lose her breath. At least that's what she thought.

"Yvonna…w…what did you give me?"

"I told you," she laughed.

"Well…h…how c…c..come, I can't breathe?"

"I don't know baby. Don't try to fight it though. You'll make things worse."

When she pulled her last breath, and passed out on the couch, Yvonna walked over to Caven and kissed him on the lips.

"You didn't tell me about the letter," he said as he stood up straight and wrapped his arms around her.

"I know," she winked. "It was a little something I thought of last night. Nice touch right?" She boasted.

"Great idea," he smiled as she ferociously tongue kissed him. The kissed lingered for a few more seconds and then he screamed, "Ouch! What the fuck was that?!" He continued rubbing his arm.

"The same thing I gave her," she replied backing away from him.

"But why the fuck would you inject me with heroin?" he asked as he fell on the couch, partially on Sabrina.

"Is that what you thought it was?" she laughed.

"Well what is it?"

"Cyanide poison."

"Why?" he asked angrily. "I loved you!"

"Why not?" she giggled. "Somebody has to stay and watch her for me. Plus you're too weak."

"Weak?" he repeated placing his hand on his chest. His breathing altered too.

"Yes…besides…you've become too much of a liability to me," she advised.

He gained enough energy to stand up and grab a hold of Yvonna. She hadn't counted on him having so much strength after being induced. Based on Sabrina's reaction, she figured he'd be out within a few minutes. But unlike Sabrina, Caven was a healthy man who worked out regularly, so he was able to withstand more.

When Caven got a hold of Yvonna, she fell up against the wooden table breaking it instantly. Her back was in pain as Caven placed all of his weight upon her. She fought desperately to get him off, but he was far too strong.

"You bitch!" he screamed growing weaker and weaker. "I should've known you couldn't be trusted," he continued as his hold on her neck became lighter and lighter.

Yvonna hit him in the face repeatedly but nothing. If she didn't get him off of her, she'd die next to them both.

Suddenly he stopped fighting and fell flat on his back on the floor. His eyes were wide open. Yvonna stood up straight and rubbed her throat. She made it…barely. Dusting herself off, she reached in her purse and pulled out the naked pictures of Bilal Jr. that she'd taken when she lived with Sabrina.

The pictures were normal, with the exception of the baby being without clothes in every last one of them. *Alone* the photos weren't so bad. It was the letter that added the pieces to the fake puzzle. Yvonna picked up Sabrina's left hand and placed the letter under it.

To whomever reads this,
I am so sorry for being less than a parent. I exposed my only son to a life that he never would've known otherwise. I never knew I had fantasies for him, until I met Caven. His love for boys heightened my sexual desires and made me realize that there's so much more to human sexuality. I know many people can't and won't understand this and because of it, I've chosen to take my own life and the life of my partner in this heinous crime. I only hope that you'll tell my son how much I loved him.
With love,
Sabrina.

"Well Sabrina," Yvonna said as she took a deep breath and picked up her purse and gloves. "I guess you and Bilal can be together after all."

She walked to her car, and called the police from another untraceable cell phone. Not saying who she was, she told the operator she wanted to report a murder suicide.

"I don't want to get involved! I'm just a concerned neighbor." She said.

When the call was ended, Yvonna laughed at the plan she'd formed from the *very* beginning. Poor Caven didn't see his death coming. She knew all along that eventually he would have to die. But…she'd hoped she could keep him a little while longer. Besides, he gave the bomb head. But after seeing Terrell in their hotel room, and speaking with Gabriella, she decided it was also his time to die.

Chapter Twenty-Seven

Visitor

Jhane' was skeptical but the doctor looked harmless enough. Although she let him in, she couldn't help but wonder what his true motives were. Like Yvonna, he hired a private detective to find out about her family and was brought to her.

"Thanks for inviting me over," he said as he stepped in and looked around the cozy one bedroom apartment.

Although the neighborhood was not in the safest area, the inside of her home reflected nothing but love. Huge plants hung in flower pots from the ceiling. And colorful burgundy and gold throws lay neatly along the sides of the couch to offer her visitors extra warmth if needed.

"No problem," she said as she sat down on the couch, placing the burgundy throw over her legs. "I'm not sure what I can do for you, but I'm willin' to listen."

"Well, as you already know, I'm working with Yvonna."

"Good," she responded pulling the brown cotton dress she was wearing over her knees, adjusting the throw next. "Cuz somebody's got to help her. Over the years she's gotten nothin' but worse."

Jhane' was a tall statuesque woman. You took notice of her the moment she walked in a room. She kept her hair in thin individual braids most of her life to prevent from being bothered with her real hair.

"I wanted to come over to see if you can give me any additional information regarding Yvonna's past," he continued as he sat across from her wearing an all black tailored made suit. "She's pretty evasive whenever I try to talk to her, so I was hoping you could shed some light on things."

"Isn't this like breaking the doctor patient confidentiality thingy?" she questioned. Although she was considered hood, she did know a *little* about the law.

"Yes…that's why I'm hoping our conversation will remain private."

Jhane' took a deep breath, stood up and plopped down on the green recliner instead. Once there, she rocked back and forth.

"I don't know much about her because my sister never allowed us into her home. Her husband, Yvonna's father, didn't like outsiders visiting much," she started. "And I haven't seen him since my sister died. But they've had problems from Yvonna for awhile."

"Can you tell me what sort of problems she had?" he questioned as he pulled a pen and pad out of his briefcase to take notes. Although he wasn't there for true medical reasons, he was trying to retain as much information about her as possible. After not receiving a call from Yvonna, he vowed to make every attempt to fuck up her life. And then he realized he knew nothing about her. She never talked about her past. All he knew was that her mother was burned in a house fire by some gang members. "Like what happened to her when she was a child?" he inquired.

"How much did Yvonna tell you?"

"She says she can't remember a lot," he lied. What she really told him was to mind his fucking business.

"That figures," she laughed. "She only remembers what she wants to *when* she wants to. I think she fakes a lot of her black outs too."

"Black outs?" he asked remembering the times he shared with her when she lived at their home in Baltimore. On quite a few occasions she'd flip out and a little later, not remember.

"Yeah…whenever she's confronted by somebody or something, she blacks out and conveniently forgets. If her mother didn't buy her lies, she'd blame it on somebody else. I forget the girl's name she used. I think it begins with "G" or something."

"I see," he said placing the pen in his briefcase along with the pad. "So she had a lot of problems coming up?"

"Yes."

"Do you think the death of her mother had anything to do with it?"

"No she was a mess before my sister died."

"So you don't think it had anything to do with the gang? I mean after all, that's a violent way to lose someone you love." he advised.

"Gang?" she questioned as she placed her feet flat on the floor, stopping her chair from rocking. Leaning in she said, "Is that what she told you?"

"Yes…," he advised already knowing a lie was getting ready to be revealed. "She told me that her mother was murdered by some gang members."

Jhane' burst out into laughter. "Let me tell you something," she whispered. "My sister wasn't killed by no gang. That bitch lied to you more than I thought. She died in a fire. At first we thought her husband Joe had something to do with it because they were separated yet he was over there that night. But Yvonna gave him an alibi when she said she left a candle burning. So based on her story, she was the reason my sister died. That's one of the reasons I hate her to this day.

"Oh…," he paused. "I see. I'm sorry to hear that. I didn't know."

"You wouldn't," Jhane continued. "Anything come out of her mouth is a fuckin' falsehood."

"I'm just sorry I came over here and made you relive everything all over again."

"Don't be," she advised. "All I can do is go on and protect my niece."

"She has a sister?" he asked as his mouth hung open.

"Yes, you didn't know that eitha?"

He shook his head no.

"Doesn't sound like she told you much of anything correct does it?"

"Apparently not," he said as he wondered who in the fuck he'd been living with for the past four years. "May I have a drink of water?"

"Sure," she said as she used her arms to push herself out of the chair. "You sure you don't' want a little something in it? Like vodka?"

"Actually that would be better," he smiled. He was left with his thoughts when she disappeared into the kitchen to fix the drink.

When she returned she said, "So when was the last time she came to see you?"

"Uh..the other day," he lied.

"Oh...," she said as she rocked in the chair again. "And she told you about me?"

"No," he responded as he downed over half of the drink in his glass before sitting it back on the table. "I had to find you on my own. That's why I'd like it if you keep this meeting between us."

"I will. So I guess she told you that her friend committed suicide and murdered some man too."

"No," he responded wondering what she was talking about.

"Yeah...they found her friend Sabrina and a man named Caven Journey dead in her house. Apparently she was molesting her own baby with him. It's terrible."

When Terrell heard Caven's name, he dropped his glass causing vodka to spill all over her living room floor.

"I'm so sorry," he responded as he jumped up looking for something to wipe it with. On instinct he grabbed the gold throw and used it.

"No!" she screamed.

"Oh...I'm sorry." He handed her the drenched throw and apologized over and over again.

"Don't worry," she responded as she snatched the throw and disappeared into the kitchen returning with a paper towel. "I guess you didn't know about the deaths after all."

"Uh...no, I didn't."

"Yeah. It' sad. Her son was already removed from the home because she neglected him. That's the word on the street anyway. But I don't believe a word of it," she continued sitting back in the chair. "Have a seat," she advised. When he sat down he continued. "I think Yvonna had something to do with that little situation too. It seems like since she's been back, trouble has started. Anyway, the little boy lives with his grandmother permanently now. She just so happens to be Bilal's mother too. And if you didn't know by now, Bilal was Yvonna's boyfriend before *he* died."

"He died?" he questioned.

"Yes. Supposedly Joe killed him but the cops have been trying to find him for years. A few of them even came by here recently, but I ran them off because they wanted to ask Jesse questions. She saw Bilal's murder. But I don't want her involved and I've made that clear. Hell she hasn't even told me what happened. The bottom line is, everyone around her dies."

"Are you serious?"

"Very…," Jhane advised.

Terrell couldn't believe it. He went to school to determine who should be considered medically insane yet he gave Yvonna full access to his banking accounts.

"Part of me thinks she killed Bilal and part of me doesn't. I mean, that story she told the cops about Joe losing his memory and quirking out doesn't make much sense. I think Yvonna found out that Sabrina was pregnant by him and pulled the trigger herself."

Terrell was listening but he hadn't expected to hear Caven being murdered or Yvonna being a murderer. Now he felt guilty for blackmailing Caven.

He threatened to tell Yvonna that Caven was born with both female and male organs if he didn't let him into the hotel room. So to prevent from losing her, he complied.

"Jhane, I appreciate your time," he said standing up. "But I really have to go now."

"I'm sorry," she giggled. "Did I lay too much on you?"

"No…you've actually given me everything I need." With that he stooped down and picked up his briefcase.

"Well I'm glad I could help," she smiled before she opened the door to let him out. "If you need me again, you know the number."

"I do," he continued as he shook her hand. "Have you spoke to her?"

"A few times. She's been trying to talk to Jesse and I've been avoiding her."

"I see. Well, good night, and thanks again."

When the door closed behind him, and the city air hit his face, it was then that he realized he wasn't dreaming. He'd come to the realization that he harbored a monster. He decided it wasn't worth pursuing her anymore because it was obvious that she was dangerous. So he counted his losses and headed back to Baltimore city before he also ended up dead.

Chapter Twenty-Eight

What's So Damn Important

Yvonna sat in the tub full of water attempting to relax. But since she hadn't heard from Treyana, she realized it was impossible.

Let me call this bitch one more time. She thought. Reaching for her Blackberry on the edge of the tub, she hit speed dial to call her.

"Where are you?"

"Outside of Cream's house."

"So what's going on?" Yvonna asked as she watched the white Dove soap bar float in the water. "You do it yet or what?"

"I can't hear you," Treyana said.

Yvonna glanced at her phone and saw the signal was perfect. *This bitch playin' games.* She thought.

"Treyana, don't fuck wit me. I can hear you perfectly and I know you can hear me. Now what's up with the rest of our plan?"

"I can't do it," Treyana said. "Me and Avante have been workin' on our relationship and I like having him around. He trusts me."

"Yeah but have you forgotten who made it possible?"

"No, Yvonna," she replied. "But with Sabrina killing herself, and Cream driving herself crazy over everything, I don't think now's the time to make matters worse."

"But we had a fuckin' deal bitch!" she yelled dropping her right hand in the water causing it to splash.

"Do you even care about what happened to Sabrina?"

"Did you see me at the funeral?"

Silence.

"What is wrong with you, Yvonna?"

"Don't fuck wit' me, Treyana. I'm warning you, don't fuck wit me. Or you can end up like Sabrina."

"Alright," she responded in a low tone. Treyana wasn't sure, but she had a feeling what she was capable of.

"I'll be waiting on confirmation that our plan is complete. If you don't call me in an hour, I'll let Avante know that this has all been a game. I know you wouldn't like that now would you?"

"Yous a fuckin' bitch!"

"Naw…," she giggled. "Call me bossy. Bye," she continued as she threw her phone on the bathroom floor.

Yvonna had planned the ultimate mind blower for Cream. It wasn't good enough for her that Avante had taken an apparent *new* interest in his ex-wife. She wanted her heart broken with the loss of Sabrina and her fiancé. She didn't care that the wedding was already off due to Sabrina's death. She didn't flinch when Cream told her that she had a feeling that Avante and Treyana were getting back together. She wouldn't be fully satisfied until Cream walked into the hotel room, and saw Treyana riding Avante's dick, then and only then would she be satisfied.

The plan was simple. Cream would walk into her apartment and find an envelope and a rose on the kitchen table. Treyana copied Avante's house key so she had full access to Cream's apartment and was supposed to plant it there. Upon opening the envelope, a small plastic key card would fall out and onto the floor. She'd pick it up and notice it was for the Marriott hotel. She'd place the card on the table and read the greeting card inside. It would say the following:

Cream,
    I know you probably don't trust me. And after everything that has been happening lately, I can't say that I blame you. But it's important to me that you know that I love you and still want to be your husband. Take the card, and the rose, and meet me at the Marriott downtown. Forever in Love
Avante

So what the handwriting looked nothing like Avante's. Cream would be too excited to realize it. All she wanted was Avante back. And Yvonna was counting on it.

Two hours later Yvonna received a text message saying *"It's done. I hope you enjoy your life in hell because that's exactly where you'll be going!"*

Yvonna laughed the message off. Going to hell was the least of her worries. With everyone else taken care of, Dave was all that was left.

When her Blackberry began to ring off the hook, she knew Treyana had executed the plan correctly. Cream had called her a total of thirty times in fifteen minutes. She didn't even bother answering. She just listened to the message and laughed.

Yvonna, it's me, Cream. I lost him forever! He's back with Treyana and I don't want to live anymore. She set me up Yvonna! I'm so hurt! Can you please talk to me? Please! I don't know what else to do.

I hope she does kill herself. Yvonna thought. *That would be the bow on top of my gift.*

Now out of the tub, she walked into the hotel bedroom, reached for the list in the dresser drawer and crossed Cream's name off. Sitting back on the sofa, she exhaled.

"So what are you gonna do?" Gabriella asked as Yvonna sat on the sofa in the hotel room.

"I don't know," she said as she played with the cold chicken fingers on the plate next to her. "They didn't mention my name in the investigation, so I ain't gonna do shit right now." She was referring to Sabrina and Caven's murder.

"You know it's just a matter of time before the cops run into the doctor right?" Gabriella said as she sat Indian style on the floor in front of her. "We might have to kill his ass too."

"I thought you said we may need him?"

"I changed my mind."

"Why are you so obsessed with killing people?"

"I'm not obsessed," Gabriella laughed. "I just happen to believe that some people don't deserve to live on the face of the earth, especially if they're runnin' their mouths like Sabrina and your doctor friend."

"Why doesn't he just go back to Baltimore?!" Yvonna griped.

"That's what the fuck I'm saying," Gabriella said as she lie flat on her back and wiggled her toes.

They didn't know that he was already home. Yvonna was silent as she thought about Gabriella, and how she always managed to get her to do things she might not have otherwise. With everything going on, she forgot about the murder at Friday's and decided to ask.

"Gab," Yvonna said in a low voice.

"Yes I did it," Gabriella responded sitting up straight.

"Yes you did what?" Yvonna questioned shocked at her response.

"Yes I did murder that bitch! And she fought like a dog too."

"How did you know I was gonna ask you that?"

"I know everything about you," Gabriella laughed as she sat on the couch and wrapped her arm around Yvonna's neck. "I thought you knew that already. You and I are one."

Yvonna produced a light hearted giggle. But she finally got it, her best friend was nothing more than a cold hearted murderer. So what did that make her? They talked for a few moments before Gabriella left her alone to swim in her own thoughts. She could see a bad ending for herself if she didn't wrap things up quick.

Needing to talk to someone she loved, she attempted to call her sister again.

"Yes, Yvonna?" Jhane responded seeing her number on the caller ID.

"Can I *please* speak to Jesse?" She waited for her response. When she gave it to her, her heart fell in the pit of her stomach.

"She isn't ready. Let her call you."

"Are you even telling my sister how much I miss her? Or are

you saying fuck it."

"Yes I do tell her Yvonna," she responded with as much attitude as she could muster. "And every time she says she's not ready. I know what I'll do next time," she said breathing angrily into the phone. "The next time I'll record her saying no. Maybe then you'll leave this child alone." She slammed the phone down.

As mean as her statement was, Yvonna would've loved to hear the tape just to hear her voice. Overhearing the conversation, Gabriella walked into the living room.

"I miss my sister," Yvonna cried hoping Gabriella wouldn't say anything negative. "And I want to speak to her."

"Why do you accept that shit from that Sasquatch lookin' bitch anyway?! She's your fuckin' sister! Go over there and talk to her and if she don't let you in, kick the door down!"

"I don't feel like it right now," Yvonna said as she wiped her tears. "I really want to be left alone Gabriella."

Gabriella was upset but respected her request. Before she left she said, "I'm on your side Yvonna, remember that."

Yvonna sat on the couch and cried herself to sleep.

Eventually Yvonna found her way to the bedroom to get some rest but was suddenly awoken to some shuffling in the living room area of the suite. She grabbed the sheet from the bed and wrapped it around her naked body. She figured it was Gabriella until she called her name and she didn't answer. Then she became nervous.

Walking carefully into the living room, her eyes fought hard to adjust within the darkness. She was so scared she couldn't locate the light switch. When she regained some sight, she saw four figures standing before her. Without saying anything they grabbed her, exposing her naked body.

"What the fuck is going on?! She yelled as they handled her with brut force.

They didn't respond.

"What's going on?!" she repeated as she managed to smack one of them in the face.

The minute she landed a blow someone flipped the light on and hit her so hard in the jaw her side tooth flew out.

"Next time I'll kill you." One of them said. "Get this bitch something to throw on."

Their faces were covered with ski-masks and she couldn't see them. She wondered who they were and all kinds of thoughts raced through her mind. What scared her most was the gun pointing in her direction.

One of them disappeared into her bedroom and returned with some jeans and a shirt.

"Put this on." The same one who hit her demanded.

Although she couldn't see their faces, she felt their stares as she got dressed.

"Listen, you're coming with us, if you try to bring any attention our way I'll put a bullet in your head and I don't care whose watching. You got it?"

She nodded yes.

They removed her shaken body out of the room and through the hotel lobby, barefoot. There was one on each side of her as they held her arms firmly. A few people saw her being taken out by masked men but no one bothered getting in their way.

Once in the car she said, "Can somebody please tell me what's going on?" The driver got in the front seat, someone jumped in the passenger and the other two sat on each side of her in the back.

"You'll find out in a minute bitch," one of the others finally spoke.

The hair on the back of her neck stood up as she realized exactly who the voice belonged to. She heard the same voice outside of the hotel.

"Swoopes…is that you?"

He laughed.

Chapter Twenty-Nine

What Goes Around Comes Back Double Time

*T*he run down old house smelled of piss. It was so strong that after only fifteen minutes of being inside, Yvonna wore the funk on her skin like perfume. Three of the six windows had completely been shattered and boarded up. Insects and rodents found solace inside, and termites had eaten the wooden floor frames almost completely. When she looked out of what was left of one of the windows, she could see the letters "Mart" and figured she was somewhere on Martin Luther King boulevard.

She was flat on her back, on the top of an old bed with her legs and arms spread out. The left bed post was broken so it leaned forward slightly in the front. Her ankles and wrists were tied on each corner of the bed with twine, exposing the inside of her vagina and her naked body. The same four men who kidnapped her, were now at the foot of the bed watching her. Someone had stuffed a pair of soiled underwear in her mouth and she could taste the bodily fluids from it.

"Whatz up, bitch?" Swoopes said as he walked over to the head of the bed, next to her face, and stooped down. He removed his mask so that she could see him clearly. The eye patch was still visible, and she saw three fingers missing from his right hand.

"Aghgh..aghhh..aghhh," Yvonna mumbled. It was difficult trying to speak with the underwear in her mouth. Swoopes removed them.

"Look at this whore." He said as he turned around and smiled at his boys. "I see why you had them niggas Bilal and Dave sweatin' you."

When he turned back around to look at her, she hock spit in his face and it watched it hang at the end of his nose.

Smack! Smack! He hit her twice in the face with his left hand.

"What do you want with me?" she yelled! "Whateva you gonna do, do it!"

"You think you smart don't you," he asked as he wiped the spit off his face and smeared it on hers. "That's a nasty habit you got you trouble-makin' bitch! You shoulda stayed away!"

She didn't speak. Just stared into his eyes.

"Five-O been tryin' to catch yo ass," he responded as he looked at her naked body again. "And when they started askin' questions, I knew they figured what I knew all along, that you had everything to do with Bilal's death."

"I didn't do it," she pleaded realizing that he had every intention on killing her. When she glanced a little closer at the men behind her, she saw they were wearing black jackets with YBM symbols written in red. "It was my father who killed him not me! I loved Bilal."

"Stop lyin' bitch! The only reason I let you live back then was cuz Dave begged me not to kill you. He's been on your shit for the longest! Do you realize how much money you fucked me out of? You know what they did to me?" he asked angrily. "First they threw paint thinner in my face burning my eye, and then they cut a finger off a week until I paid them in full. Look at me!" he yelled raising his patch showing his eye which looked completely white.

"So what you gonna do to me?" she asked realizing nothing she said would prevent her fate.

"Well," he said grabbing her titties covering his eye. "First I'm gonna fuck you, then I'm gonna let my boys fuck you, and then I'm gonna let Mack fuck you."

"Who's Mack?" she cried.

"Bring him in." Swoopes told one of the members. Seconds later, they brought in a huge sandy brown Great Dane who was barking crazily. "He's Mack." She tried her best to get out of the restraints but it was impossible. "And he loves fuckin' bitches." He laughed.

While she moved around wildly, Swoopes shoved his fist inside her vagina repeatedly. His tongue hung out the side of his mouth as he reveled in her pain. Yvonna lifted her chin trying to prevent from crying.

"You like that don't you?" he asked as he continued to jab her in the pussy with a balled up fist. "You ain't got to say shit because I know you do."

After that he climbed on top of her raw, and raped her unmercifully. He placed his dick in every part of her body. After he finished, the other men raped her in every way they pleased. Yvonna never experienced pain like that in all her life. It was unbearable and she wished they'd kill her instead of subjecting her to any more torture. For a second, she even thought about calling God's name. But she'd denounced him so much, that she thought he wouldn't hear her prayers.

Just when she thought it was over, and all of them bust nuts all over her body, Swoopes allowed the animal to crawl on top of the bed and hump her face. She could tell by the way he moved that he'd done this before. The animal howled as his penis hardened on her lips. Her stomach churned as she vomited all over herself when the dog reached an orgasm from his actions.

"Mack fucked the shit out that bitch!" Swoopes and the men laughed. "That's my fuckin' dog for real!" he cheered.

When the animal was done, Swoopes disappeared inside the house returning with a dirty mop. There were splinters hanging on the edges and he waved it back and forth to taunt her. If that wasn't enough, he broke it with his knee. Yvonna could only imagine what he had in store for her now. But the worse had already happened. She prayed for him to pull the trigger to put her out her misery.

"Let me put this back in your mouth," he said referring to the underwear on the floor. "I wouldn't want you screaming too loud."

"There's no need," she smiled. "I'm not gonna give you the satisfaction of screaming." Her voice was cold and calculating and it was as if she had transformed into another person.

"We'll see about that," he laughed as he forced the broken handle inside of her pussy. "You gonna cry now, bitch?" he asked just waiting for her to beg him to stop.

She remained silent, so he jammed it inside of her harder. Still she remained silent and to make matters worse, she began to laugh. When Yvonna looked at him directly in the eyes, while not so much as squinting in pain, he became terrified. He knew then that he wasn't dealing with an ordinary female.

"*She's* gonna kill you," Yvonna laughed. "It may not be now, but trust, *she* will fuckin' kill you," she continued as she laughed hysterically.

"Yo that bitch is crazy," one of the members yelled. "Finish her off and let's get the fuck out of here. I ain't got time for this bullshit," he said. He was shook.

Swoopes sat there stunned by how she was speaking to herself in the third person. He tried to laugh but couldn't. When he realized he was far from getting her to beg him to stop, they beat her until she could barely open her eyes let alone breathe.

"Let's get out of here," one of them yelled.

"You got the honey?" Swoopes asked.

"Yeah…here man!" Another one said. "Hurry the fuck up."

He twisted the top off and poured the honey all over her naked body. He wanted the rats to eat her alive. As they all walked toward the door, Swoopes took one last look at her before he left her to die, the inhumane way.

Chapter Thirty

What The Fuck Are You Saying

"*Mr. Walters! Mr. Walters...look what I got!*" yelled a ten year old boy in Dave's office doorway.

"Not now lil man," Dave responded without even looking at what he had in his hands. He was still trying to understand what Swoopes had just told him. "Come back later."

"Okay, sir." He said dejectedly walking off.

"Please tell me you just fuckin' wit me, man!" Dave said as he walked from behind his desk at the community center he ran.

"Why I gotta be playin?" Swoopes said as he sat in the chair across from his desk and placed his muddy boots on it. "I told you I was gonna wait until shit cooled off before I put it to that bitch! And shit couldn't be much cooler now."

Dave forgot about the promise Swoopes made to himself to kill Yvonna. After all, it had been years since they even discussed her or Bilal in the same breath. Dave didn't even know it was possible to hold a grudge that long over a botched up robbery. And what happened to his face and hand wasn't Yvonna's fault.

As he stood in his office, he remembered what his mother told him when he made a decision to change his life and now he wished he'd listened to her. *Son, if you really want to start all over, you have to rid yourself of all old friends.*

"Where she at!?" Dave asked trying to prevent from stealing him in his face while pushing his feet off his desk.

Swoopes immediately jumped up and said, "Why?!"

"Cuz I asked you nigga!" Dave responded stepping into his face.

"Who da fuck you think you talkin' to dawg?" Swoopes asked

as he gritted on him. "You sound like a bitch out here trippin' ova some hoe!"

"How you talkin' bout somebody cryin' when you still pissed over some cash that didn't even belong to you! Now stop playin' games and tell me where Shawty at!"

Swoopes knew Dave was ready to throw his life away for Yvonna. And it wasn't so much of *what* he said that convinced Swoopes, but *how* he said it. Because of it, he decided not to try him. He figured by the time he'd get there, she'd be dead anyway.

"She's at the dump," he said. "Where we use to hold our meetings."

Dave grabbed his keys and move toward the door as he shoved Swoopes bitch ass in the process. In a hurry, he yelled to his staff that he'd be back. He didn't have time to stop and give them details.

"Is everything okay?" Armani asked seeing how upset he was.

He was so worried about Yvonna that he didn't respond. It had been years since he'd prayed for anything. As a matter of fact, the last time he asked God for help, he was a seven year old kid. But in his car, on the way to the abandoned house, he asked God to make things okay. Because although he *acted* like he didn't care for Yvonna, he couldn't deny that he wanted her. And had felt that way ever since he first laid eyes on her when she was with Bilal.

"Yvonna hold on baby." He said out loud. "I'm coming for you."

Chapter Thirty-One

Carried

He felt as if he'd been driving forever when he finally reached the house. And when he saw the state she was in, he felt like bringing Crazy Dave back and puttin' two in Swoope's head, step brother or not.

Once at the worn out old bed, he grabbed one of the rats that had been chewing on her lower leg and threw it against the wall. Then he threw another gnawing on the inside of her thigh. He heard it squeak as it dropped to the floor and ran away. The smell of her soiled body in conjunction with the house's odors almost made him gag.

"Damn!" he yelled after seeing how badly beaten she was. Her face was swollen twice it's size, and if Swoopes didn't tell him it was Yvonna, he would've never believed it. He was pissed about letting Swoopes off so easy in his office. Had he seen the extent of the damage, he would've killed his ass.

"Yvonna," he whispered as he desperately untied her wrists and legs. "Can you hear me?"

Silence.

"Shit!" he yelled. After five minutes of being in her presence, he still couldn't get over how bad she looked. There was piss and shit all over the bed, and he wondered what the sticky substance was all over her face and body.

Dave grabbed the dirty sheet from the floor and wrapped her in it. He was thankful that she was light, so he could move her out the door quickly. He kicked over a few empty cans and loose rats as he struggled to get out the door. Once he reached his car, he knew exactly where he had to take her, to the hospital.

"Yvonna if you can hear me," he said placing the key in the ignition. "I need you to hold on. I'ma take you to the hospital."

With as much strength as she could muster Yvonna said, "P...pl..please d...don't t...take me tooo the hospital."

"But you'll die if I don't," he advised looking at her hoping she'd reconsider.

"P...pleas...ee...Dave," she said. "D...don't let them kill me." With that she passed out in the backseat of his car.

Since she chose her last words to beg him not to take her to the hospital, he wouldn't go against her wishes. He figured she was worried that Swoopes would come back to finish her off. And the way he hurt her, Dave couldn't blame Yvonna. He just hoped his decision wouldn't come back to haunt him later.

Chapter Thirty-Two

Five Days Later

Yvonna was awakened to a tugging sensation. Wiping her eyes, she sat up as straight as possible without subjecting herself to an unusual amount of pain.

"How you doin', honey?" a voice asked.

When she heard her calming tone, she was immediately put at ease. Yvonna wasn't sure but she felt she'd heard that voice before. Turning her head slightly to the left, she saw the woman who nursed her back to health after the car accident years ago.

"Neva thought you'd see me again now did cha?" Penny, the nurse asked as she made sure her pillows were fluffed and the comforter was covering her bruised body.

"No...I didn't." she smiled.

Yvonna looked around the room to see if anything looked familiar. It didn't. It was relatively small and cramped but clean. It certainly wasn't a hospital room. There were dark blue curtains on the windows, which matched the comforter on the bed. The curtains were preventing excess light from shining through and with the headache Yvonna was suffering from, she appreciated it.

She glanced at the wall in front of her and noticed roughly thirty or so boxes of tennis shoes lined up against it. The room was decorated with black furniture and there was a huge mirror on the dresser with baseball caps stacked on top of one another.

When she looked to the right, she saw a picture of Muhammad Ali in a black frame, standing over Sonny Liston during a fight. When she looked toward the left she saw the belt buckle she'd seen on Dave at Phillips Restaurant. She knew exactly where she was now.

"Honey, you okay?" she asked again placing one hand gently on her arm.

Yvonna almost jumped out of her skin. She knew Penny was there but had been daydreaming.

"I'm sawwy, child," the nurse continued, her skin just as dark as Yvonna remembered. Now she was in plain clothes instead of her uniform. "Afta all you been through, its no wonda you don't slap me for layin' hands on you."

"I'm sorry," Yvonna said. "I was just surprised. I hadn't expected you to touch me that's all."

"No problem, sweetheart," she smiled. "I'm just happy yous back. This the second time old Penny here had to bring you back to life, and cha know what, I don't mind," she winked.

"Thank you," Yvonna laughed. "Looks like you have had to save my life twice."

As she looked at the woman, she wished she was related to her in some sort of way. Despite her hearty voice and hard look, Yvonna could tell the nurse wanted to do well by her, since the first time she met her. "So what are you doing here?"

"I kept in touch wit' that young man of yours afta the accident ya'll where in togetha. He reminds me of my son who committed suicide. I miss that boy," she smiled trying hard not to cry. "So when he called me and told me you were hurt, I had to rush ova here. That man of yours loves you."

"He's not my man," Yvonna advised as she busied herself with straightening her sheet which was already perfect. She was getting embarrassed.

"Sweetheart, I know love when I sees it," she responded as she bent her head down and stared into her eyes. "And that man fuss-es ova you the same way he did afta the accident. So whether you know it or not, he is sweet on you. And judgin' by the way you smiled afta seeing his things in this here room, I'd say you are sweet on him too."

Yvonna hadn't realized her feelings for him were visible to others. She made mental notes to work on that. After all, Dave was not taken off her list and she certainly didn't want to get too comfortable with him.

"You up?" Dave said walking into the room with some colorful roses. "I thought your lil ass was neva gonna come around."

"Yeah….," she smiled as she sat up straight in the bed and attempted to fix her hair. "I guess I am."

"You hungry?" he asked as he placed the flowers next to his bed.

"Aw no you don't," the nurse interjected. "She not eatin' none of that food I see you stuffing in yo mouth round here! I gotta give her the clean bill of health first!"

"Aight, lady," he laughed. "See I was tryin' to make your first meal straight, but looks like you gonna have that soup and salad shit instead."

"Soup and salad shit?!" Penny yelled as she placed her hands on her hips and stared Dave up and down. "I have you know I makes the best food this side of town. And you weren't complainin' when I made it for you."

"I sure wasn't," he said as he planted a kiss firmly on her face. She dropped her arms by her sides and then hugged him. Yvonna could tell that he cared for her as much as she cared about him.

"Well," Penny started trying to shake the emotions she had for Dave off to tend to business. "I gots to get this young lady somethin' to eat. I got somethin' planned for you that I know you'll love," she continued as she disappeared.

When she left, Dave closed the door slightly to offer Yvonna and him some privacy.

"How you feelin'?" he asked looking her over. "You straight? You hurtin'? You need anything?"

"I'm fine…my head's killin' me though," she responded as she touched her forehead. She thought telling him about how bad her vagina hurt due to the gang rape would be too much. "I guess you know what happened right?"

"Do I know what happened?" he repeated. "Hell yeah I do! I felt like breakin' that niggas jaw for what he did to you. I decided to take a different route."

"Why you get involved?" she questioned. "I told you I can handle my own business."

"Yvonna, please," Dave said taking his cap off and adding it to the stack of the others on the dresser. She glanced at his neatly cut wavy hair.

Is there anything about him I don't like? She thought.

"You wasn't handlin' shit when I got to that house. You lucky I came when I did."

"So what you do? Kill him?"

"Naw…," he responded. "I did some shit I'm not proud of."

"Are you gonna tell me or what?"

He sat on the edge of the bed and placed his hand on her foot which was nestled under the covers.

"I had some information about a job he was gettin' ready to do. So I called a few cops who use to be on me when I was slingin'."

"So you snitched?" she asked, not pegging him for the bitch type.

"Yeah…the old me would've blasted his head off the moment he told me what happened," he responded looking up at her. "But I'm all the kids at my center got and I can't see riskin' it. They need me and I need them."

"I see," Yvonna responded slightly disappointed. She would've rather he popped him than to get the cops involved. That was the gangster in her. "What you get him on?"

"Don't worry 'bout that," he responded as he took his shirt off and threw it on the back of a chair. She smiled after realizing she did the exact same thing with her clothes. Now sitting in a plain white T he said, "The less you know the betta."

"Why you doin' all this for me?"

"Cuz you hate me that's why," he laughed.

"I don't hate you," she admitted. "Although I should. What do you want from me?" she asked from nowhere. "Nobody's eva nice unless they want somethin' so what do you want?!"

"I want you to relax. That's all I want you to do right now is relax. Can you do that for me?"

"I hope you know you not gettin' no pussy, Dave! Cuz if that's the case, you coulda left me right where you found me," she responded.

"I fucks wit you," he said as he got up, causing the bed to squeak a little. "And just so you know, you gonna wanna give me some of that pussy before everything is said and done. So I'm not even trippin' off that." He winked. "I'ma get up wit you lada." He continued as he walked out the room.

When he left she exhaled, placed her head against the backboard and looked up at the ceiling. The funny thing was, as much as she claimed he got on her nerves, she didn't want him to leave. The last time she had feelings that strong for a man was with Bilal and the connection alone scared her. And then there was the looming question, what about the list?

Chapter Thirty-Three

Try, Try Again

*D*ave held the door open wearing white boxers, no shirt and the same kind of slippers O-Dawg wore in "Boyz N The Hood".

"A witness said she's here," the white lanky female detective named Lily said as she stared at Dave's big protruding dick, not realizing how obvious she was.

"What is this about anyway?" Dave questioned as he looked between the white and the black female detectives. He already knew the answer. What he really wanted to know was who hot-boxed and told them that Yvonna was there. He wasn't sure but he had a feeling it was Swoopes. He found out from one of his peeps that Swoopes was taking a lot of heat from the information Dave had given the cops, and he hated him for it.

"Is she here or not?" The black detective interjected. She was thicker than Lily who was border line frail, but not fat. However she had ass for days. The brown pants she wore technically couldn't hold it all because the seams were starting to give way on the sides. Wearing a green shirt, she looked like a big ass bowl of pistachio ice cream. Her hair had been gelled back with that cheap ass brown stuff in a jar, and her ponytail had minimal hang time.

"Like I said…she ain't here," he replied.

"We can get a warrant you know?" the white detective added taking a peak at his dick again. She was so white she looked dead with rosy cheeks. Her hair was blonde and appeared to have been bleached too much. She had a blue suit on with a white top. In other words, both of the detectives were bum bitches.

Seeing that Lily couldn't get enough of eyeing his dick, he pretended as if he was adjusting himself. She damn near fell on her ass when she saw him maneuver the masterpiece. He laughed when he saw the look on her face.

"Let em in," Yvonna replied as she walked up behind him slowly. Her face still battered and bruised.

"You coulda told me you were gonna do that," Dave whispered after opening the door for the officers. "Got me out here lookin' crazy."

"Sorry," she whispered back. "I just want to get this shit over with."

When the detectives walked into the apartment, which was off of Addison Road in Maryland, they sat across from her on the couch and stared at Yvonna. Neither of them believed upon looking at her that she would be capable of hurting anyone let alone murder. Standing 5'6 inches, she was very thin. The plumpest parts on Yvonna's body were her breasts and ass, but even they had lost some of their substance since the rape. Her face was healing but a lot of the scars were still visible. But because they had been in law enforcement for over twenty years, they knew better than to judge a killer by their cover. Besides, they've been trying to find her ever since all of the leads to her father were dead-ends.

"So you're, Ms. Harris," Lily said.

"Yes...I am, and you are?"

"I'm Lily and this is, Shonda," she advised. "We're with the D.C. Police Department's Homicide division."

"So," she said exhaling. "What do ya'll want from me?" Yvonna sat on the loveseat, and pulled her blue robe closed.

"We want to ask you some questions about your father," Lily responded.

"What kind of questions?"

Dave didn't say much, he wanted to sit down but the MOD squad had the couch on lock and Yvonna was in his favorite chair. But he certainly wasn't leaving her side.

"Well as you know we've been investigating the death of Bilal Santana," Shonda added.

"I'm quite aware of who Bilal is," she spat. She was mad at the way Shonda said it, as if Yvonna didn't know his name. "So tell me what you want from me and stop wasting my time."

"I know you're upset," Shonda replied. "But you have to understand that we've given you more than enough time to grieve, yet Mrs. Santana still hasn't received closure regarding the murder of her son. If you're upset, you can imagine how she feels."

"Oh so I don't deserve to grieve after the fact? Not only did I witness it, but I also lost somebody who meant a lot to me...my fiancé."

"I understand," Lilly interjected. "But we still need to close this case."

"Ya'll said you had some questions for me," she paused. "So what's up?!"

"Is this your engagement ring?" Shonda asked showing the ring she left after shitting on Bilal's grave. "Someone destroyed his gravesite and we found this. Bernice said it was yours."

"Well it's not," she lied. Dave eyed the ring and knew it was hers after seeing it in the hospital the night of the murder.

"Where is your father?" Lily asked retrieving a small white pad from the inside of her navy blue blazer.

"I told you I don't know. I haven't seen him in months."

"*Months*?" they said together looking at each other to be sure they heard Yvonna correctly. "What do you mean months?" Lily continued.

"He popped up one day while I was with a friend."

"Where were you?" Shonda questioned.

"With a friend," Yvonna repeated.

"Don't be a smart ass," Shonda advised. "It's not cute."

"Well I can't remember," she said under her breath.

"But you do remember you were with a friend?" Lily stated as if she didn't believe her.

"Are you gonna continue to play games or are you gonna tell us what we need to know?" Shonda asked.

"I told you what the fuck I knew! I seen him a few months back! Now if ya'll stop wastin' my time and do your fuckin' jobs, maybe you'd find him!" Yvonna yelled.

"Look ya'll gotta leave," Dave said after seeing Yvonna becoming upset. "I know ya'll can see she's hurt."

"Yeah…what happened?" Shonda asked.

"Don't bother," Yvonna replied as she stood up walked toward Dave's bedroom and slammed the door.

"I guess you already know we'll be back with a warrant," Lily advised.

"For what? I let you in," Dave replied.

"Just because we can," Shonda smiled.

"Well you can come back with whateva the fuck you want. Ain't nobody runnin' from ya'll's punk asses anyway!"

They were so upset that they couldn't wait to leave, but both of them knew it was just a matter of time before they'd come back. And when they did, they'd be coming with a car to transport one if not both of them to the precinct.

Chapter Thirty-Four

The Approach

*T*he kids leaving the bus stop looked like a blurred rainbow because of the rush they were in and the colorful back packs and clothing they wore. Still, with all of the running around, Yvonna was able to spot her sister.

"Jesse," Yvonna said as she caught up with her right after she got off the school bus. She found out what school she went to, and made it her business to catch her before she went into the house. She had a feeling something would be happening to her soon and she wanted to make things right with Jesse…in person.

Even with one arm, Yvonna couldn't get over how pretty Jesse was. Her natural brown hair fell down to her waist and she was amazed at how much she looked like her. Yvonna smiled remembering how her hair color used to be the same. She hated it when she was younger because their mother always called it dirty brown. And to Yvonna, anything "Dirty" was not good.

Yvonna's heart broke when she noticed Jesse was desperately tying to conceal the fact that one of her arms was missing. She wore it tucked under a red long sleeve jacket and she noticed it wasn't designer.

What the fuck is Jhane doing with the money I give her? Yvonna thought. She sent no less than three thousand a month and Jesse should be wearing designer fashions not clothing fitting of bamma bitches. *I'll get Jhane's ass before my life is over.*

"Yvonna?" Jesse said as she looked at her as if she were a ghost. "What are you doing here?" She was speaking to her as she walked backwards.

Kids ran all around them yet they appeared to be the only ones standing on the face of the earth.

"I've missed you," Yvonna responded. She was dressed down compared to how she used to dress. She wore no makeup and her hair was brushed back. No mousse. No nothing. "Why don't you want to speak to me sis?"

"Cuz?"

"Cuz what?" she asked as she walked along with her.

"Cuz you scare me," Jesse said as she stopped walking.

Yvonna couldn't believe what her sister was saying. She wondered what it was about herself that made the only person she loved scared of her.

"What do you mean I scare you?"

"Yvonna, I gotta go. I'll call you. I promise." She lied.

"No," she said as she grabbed her hand, adding a smile to lessen her obtrusiveness. "You can talk to me. Tell me what I've done."

Jesse looked to the ground before looking up at her sister. "I remember, Yvonna. I remember everything," Jesse said in a low voice.

"And so do I," Yvonna responded as tears dripped down her face. "It's supposed to be you and me against the world because we've been through everything together."

"No! I mean I remember everything *you* did."

"What do you mean?"

Jesse turned around and walked toward her door which was only a few houses down. "Please leave me alone. I don't want to hurt your feelings." She almost reached the door but Yvonna pulled her. "I know how you are when you're mad. You need help, Yvonna," Jesse responded. "Please go get help. The doctors can help you. I know it. But you have to go see them first."

"Fuck her!" Gabriella said right by her side. Yvonna didn't realize she was there. Yvonna's eyes got two sizes too big when she heard her swear in front of her sister.

"Don't say that," Yvonna replied. "She's my sister."

"But if she wants to act like you ain't been lookin' out for her I wouldn't trip off of that bitch! Sister or not! You got me. You don't need nobody else."

Yvonna couldn't believe Gabriella was saying all of the things she was in front of Jesse, knowing full well how much her sister meant to her.

"So what's *her* name?" Jesse asked as tears fell down her eyes. "Huh?"

"I said, what's her name?" she repeated. "Is it Shelby? The one that use to hit on me? Or is it Charmaine? Or maybe you're daddy again?"

"Don't listen to that bitch!" Gabriella screamed. "Let's leave!"

"Shut the fuck up Gabriella!"

"Gabriella," Jesse repeated as she cried hard. "The one that killed mama." Yvonna stood there looking at her sister with pain and confusion.

"You need help Yvonna. You're not daddy, your not Shelby and you're not Gabriella. You're one person! You can't fool me no more! I know! Stop blaming everybody else and get help! Please!" With that Jesse took off running up the steps leading to her apartment building. Before entering she stopped and said, "I saw a movie about you once. It's called *A Beautiful Mind*. You should see it." And then she was gone.

Yvonna stood there in silence. *A beautiful mind? And what does she mean I'm not Gabriella? I never said I was.* Yvonna thought. Her sister's actions were beyond weird and Yvonna didn't understand them fully. And when she turned around to confront Gabriella she was gone.

Chapter Thirty-Five

Finally

Either they don't know, don't show or don't care about what's going on in the hood. Dave was sitting on his couch looking at Boyz N The Hood on DVD for the hundredth time when Yvonna came bursting in the door. Startled, he reached in between the cushions and grabbed his 45. Although he was out of the game, he kept a little something with him just in case.

Realizing it was her, he tucked his piece under the couch and ran over to her. She was upset at what recently happened with Jesse. Prior to now she always thought it was her aunt who was keeping them apart. But now with her own ears, she heard her only sister say she wanted nothing to do with her...*ever.*

"What's goin' on?" Dave asked as he moved out of her way, allowing Yvonna to throw herself to the couch.

"I don't want to talk about it!" she cried as she hid herself within the pillows of the large sofa. "Anyway you wouldn't understand."

"Try me," he said as he sat on the left side of the sofa, as she curled up tight on the right.

"I just told you that you wouldn't understand," she said, her voice mumbled.

"Get up, Yvonna," he demanded.

"No!"

"Get up, Yvonna," he yelled again.

"No...leave me alone!" she replied crying hysterically.

Unable to take anymore of her bullshit, he grabbed her by the arm forcing her to sit up straight.

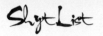

"Get off me!" she yelled hitting him in his chest. "Don't put your fuckin' hands on me!"

Like a rock, he allowed her to unleash on him until she fell helplessly in his arms. And when she did, he embraced her tightly.

"Why doesn't she want to see me? She's the only family I care about! I love her so much, Dave. She's my baby sister!"

Since Yvonna had been staying with him, he sometimes heard her talk to herself about missing her sister. Outside of those few times she never verbally told him anything about Jesse.

"It's gonna be aight, Shawty," he said stroking her back as she held on to him tightly.

"I don't understand! I just don't understand," she continued.

Dave remained silent. He knew drilling her about what happened right now wouldn't make things any better. If he wanted to help, all he had to do was continue what he was doing, holding her. His plan worked because as the seconds went by, she cried less and less. And soon, instead of sobbing about her sister's rejection, her lips met his.

There was so much passion between them, that neither saw it coming. If they had, perhaps they would've been more gentle. Instead, he pulled her closely to him and kissed her deeply as if he'd just gotten out of jail. And she did the same.

The cologne he was wearing was intoxicating. She breathed him in. He needed her. This wasn't in her plan. She wasn't prepared. How could she get back at a man who was driving her wild?

When he placed his body over hers, they stretched out on the couch. Yvonna knew Dave was just what she needed to get over her problems. At least for now, like a drug, he was the *other* alternative. And when she felt him….inside of her, she felt as if she was spinning.

"D….Dav…vee….you…feel soooo good!" she cried out.

She couldn't help what she was feeling. The truth was she'd been feeling Dave for some time now. As a matter of fact, she was feeling him back when Bilal was alive. She used fighting with him as a means to hide what was already obvious to some people, including Bilal. His aggressiveness, the way he bossed her around, were all turn-ons. She could do nothing with a weak ass man. But with Dave, she felt she could conquer the world.

With each stroke he made, she became wetter and wetter. Her juices gently fell between her legs as he fucked her with precision. They were one. His mouth covered hers and their tongues did a dance of their own.

"Turn around," he instructed.

She did.

Yvonna felt lost when his dick left her extra wet pussy. The soreness she experienced from the rape was diminished due to how she felt for him. And when he found her again, she was quickly satisfied as he went as deep as he could without causing her any pain.

"Damn," he finally yelled as he used her waist as handle bars to ride her phat ass. "I didn't know you felt like this."

Yvonna said nothing, she couldn't. Dave was hitting all the right spots and she was sure Bilal had mentioned to him the way she liked it. Why else after only the first time they'd made love, would he tell her to turn around to hit it from the back?

When she tried to remind herself that she hated him, she thought of something else. Fucking Dave was another way she was sure she'd gotten revenge on Bilal, even if it wasn't in her *original* plan. And then she ran her tongue up the tattoo he had with Bilal's name on it. The one he'd gotten after Bilal was killed.

"I'm bout to bust!" he yelled as his strokes became swifter and swifter.

"Mmmmmmmm," Yvonna moaned. "Me tooooo. Please don't stop."

He didn't stop. He released. She released and they both moaned out their indiscretions. Needless to say, Yvonna was in a far better mood than she was before Dave gave her 10 inches of rock hard dick.

"What did we just do?" she asked as she lie in front of him on the couch. His arms holding her tightly while his body pressed against hers.

"You know what we just did," he joked. "Don't act like you didn't feel me tappin' that ass a minute ago."

"Seriously," she responded, her voice low. She was already having regrets.

"We stopped playin' games, Yvonna. That's what happened." She was silent. "You got a problem with that?" He asked.

"No," she paused. "For some reason I don't."

"Then that's all that matters."

Chapter Thirty-Six

Sweet Revenge

*T*he interrogation room was dark with the exception of the light shining above the table. Detectives Lily and Shonda were excited about the call they received while at lunch. Bernice and Cream agreed to speak to them regarding Bilal's case. In addition, they claimed to have someone else for them to speak with who would be invaluable to the investigation. Bernice and Cream also mentioned that they had some information about the video clip circulating on the news regarding the murder at Friday's.

"Please…have a seat," Lily advised Bernice and Cream.

"Thanks," Bernice said. She had bags under her eyes and it appeared as if she hadn't slept in months. "I appreciate it," she continued as her chair made a screeching noise as it drug against the floor.

Cream helped Bernice into her seat, before taking her own. Her hair was tied loosely in a ponytail and strands of blonde hair sat messy on her head. She was already thin but had dropped an additional fifteen pounds since Yvonna came back into the picture. She was visibly shaken and on the verge of crying.

"Can I get you anything, Cream?" Shonda asked noticing her mood.

"No…I'm good," Cream said looking at Bernice. "Just want to get this over with that's all."

"Okay," Lily said as she neatly stacked some papers together. "Let's get started. First my name is Lily Alvarez-Martin and this is my partner, Shonda Wright."

Bernice and Cream smiled at them both.

"When we got your message today," Lily continued. "I must say I was very surprised. We've been following this case for quite some time now and all of our leads ended up dead."

"Yeah," Shonda interjected. "Seems like this chick has more people protecting her then we thought."

"I don't think that's the case," Bernice added.

"What do you mean?"

"The protecting her part," Bernice continued. "Some people are just frightened of her."

"Tell us more," Lily added.

Bernice took a deep breath and squeezed Cream's hand. "I think we should bring her in now," Bernice said to Cream in a low voice.

"Me too," Cream advised.

"Bring who in?" Shonda asked.

"Her sister…Jesse." Bernice said.

With that Cream stood up and opened the door. Jhane' was standing on the other side holding her niece's hand.

"Please…please come in," Shonda said mouth wide open.

Upon seeing Jesse, the little girl they'd been trying to talk to since Bilal was murdered, they realized more was going to be revealed today than all the years of investigation they put together. Lily and Shonda had stopped by Jhane's house awhile ago and Jhane ran them off the porch the moment they stepped foot onto it. But after Yvonna scared Jesse by showing up at the house, Jhane decided it was time to talk to the detectives. When the detectives got over the initial surprise of Jesse being there, they settled down to listen to her talk.

"My sister's been sick for awhile," Jesse started her voice low and shaken. To be ten going on eleven, Jesse was very well spoken. "I remember a lot, even though it was a long time ago. Like when Daddy used to come into our room and stick his thingy inside of Yvonna's mouth and private. One time I heard her cry so loud I got scared. Just put my head under the pillow and hid. One day she went to tell Mommy." she continued looking up at Jhane.

"Go head, honey," Jhane responded. "Tell them everything."

Jesse took a deep breath and looked up at Lily and Shonda with her big pretty eyes.

"When she did tell about what daddy did to her, mommy told her to stop telling lies. She told her that Daddy would never do anything like that to her. Yvonna came rushing back into our room crying real hard that night. I thought Mommy would come in and make everything better, but she didn't."

That dreadful night

Yvonna ran into the room crying after her mother called her a liar. Throwing herself onto the bed, she started having a violent tantrum. Pushing things off the dresser and to the floor was the only way she could express how she felt.

"Why does this have to happen to me?" she cried to herself. "Why!"

Jesse watched the entire thing as her older sister sat up in the bed and proceeded to have a conversation alone. Although it wasn't the first time she'd seen it, it was definitely one of the times Jesse would never forget.

"You gonna let that bitch make you cry?" Yvonna said to herself.

"Well what should I do?" she asked herself.

"You should make her pay." she responded.

"I don't want to, Gabriella."

"Either you do it, or I'ma do it!"

"I can't do this," Yvonna cried to herself some more.

"Well let me take over."

Not saying another word, Yvonna got up, walked to the basement and returned with a bottle of lighter fluid. As if she was on autopilot, she spread the fluid all around the house starting with the basement first. Within minutes, the house was fully inflamed.

Yvonna returned to her room to help her sister Jesse out, claiming it must've been her father who started the fire. He'd come over that night to talk to their mother because he didn't live there. She'd put him out suspecting he had another woman. After an argument, he left before the fire started.

As Yvonna helped Jesse out the house, she acted as if she had no recollection about the fire she started. A frightened Jesse grabbed her brown teddy bear and followed her sister out the door and they waited for the fire department to arrive.

~~~~~~

Back At The Police Station

The detectives sat in awe at how Jesse ran down all of the events of that night.

"So your sister was talking to herself? Like she was another person?" Shonda asked.

Jesse nodded her head yes.

"Did she ever do it again?"

Jesse nodded her head yes and began to explain.

"Well…after the police came, Yvonna told them that she must've left candles burning. After that we stayed with Daddy at his other lady's house."

"Other lady?" Lily repeated.

"Yeah…Daddy had another lady named Pie. So when Mommy died, we went to stay with Pie. Yvonna hated her and I did too. She was mean and treated us bad when daddy wasn't around. So when Yvonna threatened to tell Pie that he use to stick his thingy inside of her, Daddy said he would move us so we went to look for another apartment, the one Bilal got killed in. But Daddy said we couldn't move right away because he was waiting on his war check."

"War check?" Lily repeated again.

"Yeah…he was receiving a disability check from the army," Jhane added realizing her niece didn't know what it was for.

"Oh…I see. Please continue," Lily said.

"But the night we were supposed to leave, Yvonna and daddy were gone all day. Late at night, Yvonna came back to Pie's house without Daddy. She was acting like Gabriella again. I asked her where he was but she didn't tell me. Pie kept asking Yvonna too and finally she told her he was leaving her. She didn't believe Yvonna at first, but eventually she left us alone.

"Anyway, we moved that night, me and Yvonna by ourselves. For weeks I didn't see daddy and one day Yvonna said Daddy was home but he didn't want to talk to me or her. I couldn't understand why, but I didn't say anything. Daddy's room was always locked and Yvonna wouldn't allow me to talk to him. She'd say he was sleep or didn't want to be disturbed. I always thought Yvonna was lying. But one time I heard her in his room talking, and at first I thought Daddy was home. I was happy because I kinda missed him. But when I heard Yvonna's voice go deep one time, and then normal the next, I knew she was talking to herself again. I was scared. I stayed away from the room like she told me to, but I knew something bad musta happened to Daddy because Yvonna was pretending to be him."

Everyone looked at each other. This was the first time Jhane' had ever heard her niece tell the story and Bernice and Cream couldn't believe their ears either. Jhane thought all this time Joe was just being a bum and avoiding the family. Yvonna had everyone fooled. He wasn't even around.

"Well," Shonda said breaking the silence. "Did you two live alone?"

"Yeah...Yvonna took care of us by cashing daddy's checks at a liquor store. And she had this crackhead lady enroll me in school. She pretended to be my mommy."

"Anything else?" Shonda asked.

"Yeah...I remember the night Bilal was killed too."

~~~~~~

The Morning Bilal Was Killed

Bilal was fast asleep when Yvonna heard his phone vibrate. Jesse woke up the moment she saw her sister move. She could never really sleep if Yvonna was awake. She was always terrified something would happen.

"Bilal...Bilal...get up and get your phone," Yvonna said nudging him.

Bilal was out cold. If he had sex before he went to bed, getting him up early in the morning was out of the question.

Reaching over him, Yvonna decided to answer the phone instead. But when she grabbed it off the nightstand, she saw a text message. It read the following,

Bilal...I know you're probably with Yvonna, but I'm hopin' you get this in time. Please don't marry her. What about our baby? I know I'm not as pretty as her, but I'll make you so much happier. Please call me.

Yvonna read the message and snapped. She didn't realize that most of the time, her psychotic episodes were triggered by major events. Other times it would happen all on its own or when she needed something or somebody to talk to. She developed this coping mechanism after her father raped her repeatedly as a baby.

Like someone had entered her body, Yvonna walked into the room supposedly belonging to her father, and lifted a shot gun from the closet.

Returning to the room, Yvonna aimed at Bilal but Jesse moved quickly startling her and caught the first stray bullet. Next she cocked, pulled and blasted Bilal's head off.

As she had before, Yvonna ranted off like she was her father and herself at the same time. When a few minutes passed, she returned to her normal self, with no memory of what happened, and called the police.

Back At The Police Station

After hearing Jesse's account, they realized even more that Yvonna needed help. And most of all she needed to be caught, if not she was sure to kill again.

"Well...," Shonda said still trying to take everything in. "We need to bring in Yvonna now."

"Yeah...and in a hurry too," Lily advised.

"Do you need us anymore?" Jhane said. "It's really late and I'd like to get Jesse home. She has school tomorrow."

"No...no...you're free to go," Lily advised.

Jesse and Jhane stood up to leave. Gripping Jesse closely, Jhane let her know how proud she was of her.

"Before you leave," Lily said stopping them at the door. "I want you to know how brave you are, Jesse. What you did today was the right thing."

For the first time in a long time, Jesse smiled, and walked out with her aunt.

Sabrina and Cream waited nervously to tell their story. If Jesse could be so brave, certainly they could too. Cream started first and went on to tell them how things had been messed up ever since Yvonna returned to town. She stated that before she came back, she was engaged and getting married. But now she was lonely and her wedding was called off. What really let them know something was up was what Bernice had to say. She explained how the same man who was murdered with Sabrina, was the same man who showed up at the party with Treyana and at her house with the pictures.

Bernice eventually went to approach Treyana. At first she gave her a hard time saying she didn't want Yvonna on her bad side. But after hearing that she could be implicated in a murder investigation if she didn't speak, Treyana didn't have a problem telling Bernice everything she knew.

"Also," Cream started. "The tape going around about the murder at Fridays, we believe that's Yvonna too."

Shonda smiled because she had already expected that but her notion was thrown out the window by her captain.

"Can we see it again to be sure?" Cream asked still hoping her beliefs were wrong.

The detectives took everything they said down, and presented the video of Jasmine McDonald, also known as Freckles being murdered. The moment they saw the shape of her body, and the new haircut she sported, they all knew right away it was Yvonna.

"We got her," Lily said as she called her boss. "Let's get the warrant for her arrest."

Chapter ThirtySeven

Confrontation

"*I don't know where she is?*" *Dave told the detectives as he* held the door open.

"Can we come in?" Lily asked.

"Naw…," he paused. "I'm in the middle of somethin'."

"What if we have this?" Shonda said flashing a warrant in his face.

With that, they pushed open the door, and made themselves comfortable in his apartment, along with three uniformed cops.

"Check the back rooms," Shonda advised. "And if you think she may be hidin' under something rip that shit up."

Dave felt like fucking Shonda up. That's why he hated cops sometimes. He felt many of them didn't know how to handle their authority.

After fifteen minutes of ruining his place they finally said, "Stop playin' games, Dave! Where the fuck is she?!" Shonda asked throwing all professionalism out the window.

"Bitch, I told you I don't know where she is!" Dave yelled not giving a fuck about them being cops. "I ain't her fuckin' keeper!"

"So now you're insulting an officer?" Lily asked already knowing the answer to her question.

"If the fuck you can't treat me with respect, I can't treat you with none either."

"You don't know who you're dealing with, Dave," Lily warned. "She's not the person she makes herself out to be."

"I'll take my chances," he advised.

When they realized she really wasn't there, and that he wasn't giving any information about her whereabouts, they promised to return later. They didn't bother telling him that a stakeout had already been set up outside his building. They figured he'd find that out if he happened to show up with Yvonna. And then they could get them both.

Chapter Thirty-Eight

Now What

"Okay," Yvonna said wiping the tears from her eyes. "I'ma go."

"You sure? I got people in New York that can hide you out for awhile," Dave said as they sat in his car outside of a Laundromat. The moment the cops showed up at his apartment, he drove up there to let her know not to come home. He had to ditch the cops who were tailing him first, hoping he'd lead them to Yvonna. They must've been rookies because the shake off was easy.

She was washing their clothes and they had plans to go out and enjoy the rest of their day later. But those plans would be cancelled.

"I *gotta* go, Dave," she said looking down at some loose change on the floor of his car. "Plus I don't want you involved in all of this."

"Fuck that! I'm already involved," Dave said. The idea of losing her right after he got her had him fucked up.

Yvonna smiled sensing how much he cared about her, "If we want to ever have a start, I have to turn myself in. You seen 'em. They gonna always be lookin' for me and I'm tired of living like this."

"Shit!" he let out. "Why can't they just find your father and leave us the fuck alone?"

Yvonna placed her hand on his face and said, "I'm sorry I got you in all of this. I really am." They kissed as if it would be their last time.

"I'm goin wit you," he said trying to pull himself together. "And I'ma get you the best lawyer money can buy."

"Thanks...but can you take me somewhere first?"

"No doubt," he responded, scared at the chance of losing her. "Where we goin'?"

"I got to find out if something my sister said to me the other day was true," she said breathing out. "Have you ever heard of the movie, 'A Beautiful Mind'?"

He laughed a little at first before seeing she was serious.

"Uh...yeah...ain't that the movie about the dude that saw people all the time?"

Her heart dropped.

"I don't know," she said shrugging the eerie feeling off. "Can you take me where I need to go now?"

"Let's roll," he said as he put the car in drive. "Just show me the way."

Chapter Thirty-Nine

Now You'll Know

"*Let me go to the bathroom first,*" Yvonna told Dave *as* they sat in the waiting room of the doctor's office.

"Okay."

When Yvonna went into the bathroom, she placed both of her hands on the wet porcelain sink and cried. Wearing no make-up, jewelry or designer clothes, she cried out her soul. When she started crying more heavily than she thought, she turned on the water to muffle the sound.

"Why is this happening to me?" she asked herself in the mirror. Her grey New York T-shirt wet with tears.

Just then she heard a toilet flush and out came Gabriella from a bathroom stall wearing a two piece red Juicy outfit.

"Gabriella?" Yvonna said through the mirror. "What are you doing here?"

"I'm here to see the doctor."

"Why?" Yvonna asked finally turning around. "What do you want from him?"

"I'm doing something you're too afraid to do."

"Doing something I'm too afraid to do?" Yvonna repeated. "I'm not afraid to do anything. I've hurt too many people and I'm tryin' to make things right."

"You sound stupid, Yvonna!" Gabriella spat as she walked up to the mirror and grabbed her MAC compact from the matching Juicy purse that hung on her shoulder. "You're letting that brat ass sister of yours put into your head that's something wrong with you. If you ask me, she's the one who has a problem. Look at everything you've done for her. Don't do this, Yvonna! Don't go in there and let that doctor tell you I'm not real!" Gabriella begged.

"I...I...gotta go," Yvonna said trying to walk out.

"P....pl...pllllease!" Gabriella screamed. "Since we were kids it's been just me and you. We all we need!"

"I have to get better," Yvonna cried.

"You'll be sorry!" Gabriella threatened as Yvonna walked out of the bathroom. "You'll be sorry!"

Chapter Forty

Revelation

"Yvonna?" *he said looking as if he just saw a ghost.* "What are you doing here?"

"I need your help," she said softly.

"Well you have enough of my money to get all the help you need. So what the fuck you want from me now?"

"Come on, man," Dave interjected as he and she both stood outside of the Terrell's office door. "She's coming out here to ask for your help. Hear her out."

Against his better judgment he opened the door. Because although she ripped him off, he was still intrigued by everything he'd heard from the people in her life.

"What's up Yvonna?" he asked taking his seat.

"I don't know how to say this," she said as Dave held her hand tightly. "I think something's wrong with me."

"And you need me to tell you that?" he asked.

"Are you gonna help her or not?!" Dave yelled more then willing to steal his ass in the face.

"Go ahead, Yvonna," he said looking at Dave and then at Yvonna.

"My sister said something and I need to know if it's true."

When she said that, she noticed the picture of her in a gold frame still sat on the shelf behind him. When he realized what she was looking at, he turned around and placed it face down. He was embarrassed that he even still had it up. Truth be told, he was still in love with her.

"You saw Jesse?" he asked as he turned around to face her again. He thought her statement was weird considering Jhane' made it clear that she wanted to keep them apart.

"Yeah….hold up," she said remembering something major. "Up until now, I never even told you I had a sister."

"Like I said in the hotel," he responded in between fondling with some papers on his desk. "If you didn't give me back my money, I had all intentions on ruining your life. But I soon realized you weren't worth it."

Dave was hearing a lot of this for the first time. Yvonna didn't let him in on anything prior to this moment. She figured if he still wanted to be with her after hearing everything, it was on him.

"I'm sorry," Yvonna replied. "I really am. I was wrong for everything I did to you."

"That's not good enough, Yvonna," he said loosening up his royal blue and gold tie. "I wanted to marry you. I guess all you like is thugs," he continued looking at Dave. "Cause it's obvious I'm wasn't good enough for you."

"Easy, Slim," Dave warned.

"You were supposed to be my wife," Terrell responded ignoring Dave's comment.

It was then that Dave knew he was the one she talked about marrying when she first came to town.

"I would not have been good enough for you," she replied. "You deserve better."

"I know…so why don't you tell me why I should help you. As a matter of fact, give me *one* reason I should do *anything* for you." She looked at Dave and then down at her fingers.

"I'm turning myself in later today. I killed Sabrina and Caven and I think I hurt some other people too. So I'm asking you…no begging you to help me find out the truth. About my past."

Dave and Terrell were stunned. No one expected her to come clean like she had, but she needed to tell the truth for herself too. And now Terrell had confirmation that she murdered Caven.

"Okay…," he said feeling uneasy. "How do you want my help?"

"I read in one of your books, that hypnotism works when dealing with the past. Is that true?"

"Sometimes…but you have to be open to it," he responded.

"And everybody isn't.

Clearing her throat she said, "Okay...well I think I'm open enough, and I'd like your help."

"Why do you think hypnotism will work?" he questioned. "You've already admitted to the murders."

"Well...have you ever heard of the movie, 'A Beautiful Mind'?" she asked him.

"Of course...," he paused. "It was based on a true story," Terrell said. "He had Schizophrenia."

"Schizophrenia...,"Yvonna repeated. "It wasn't the first time she'd heard that name. When she was a child an old women told Yvonna's mother that she exhibited some of the behaviors. But since Schizophrenia wasn't as popular as some other mental illnesses and virtually unheard of with African American people, Yvonna was put off as being "Crazy". "Well...whatever it is...I need to understand why it's affecting me."

They talked some more before she finally convinced him of what she wanted done. The entire session was recorded. Dave and Terrell were shocked at what they'd heard.

While under hypnosis, Dave and Terrell found out that transforming into one of her alter ego's was how she committed *most* of the murders.

They learned that she murdered her mother, Bilal, Theodorus, Caven, Sabrina and the girl at Fridays. She could easily be labeled as a serial killer.

But what really shocked them was the murder of her father. Yvonna lured her father to a landing near a large body of water in D.C. She convinced him that she wouldn't fight with him anymore, and that she wanted to please him sexually. Turning herself into Gabriella, while in her father's car, she gave him oral sex. And when she was done, she put a bullet in his head, threw the car into drive, and watched it disappear into the water. Afterwards, she hitchhiked back to Pies to get Jesse. They still hadn't found his body to that day.

After hearing about her sordid past and how her father abused her for all those years, Terrell decided to help her by testifying in court. And suddenly Yvonna had hope.

Chapter Forty-One

A Jury Of Peers

*T*errell sat in the courtroom with confidence as he spoke in Yvonna's defense.

"Yvonna has the most severe case of Multiple Personality disorder, I've ever seen in my entire career."

"And how long have you been practicing Dr. Shines?" Larry Taylor, Yvonna's attorney questioned.

"Fifteen years."

"Can you explain her condition please?"

"Yes. When I first saw her, I thought she was schizophrenic. But upon further research, I changed my diagnosis immediately. Because Yvonna always desired her father's love, she never accepted the fact that he was a sexual predator. And that led to-,"

"I object!" Peter Dice, the prosecutor interrupted. "Mr. Harris is not on trial here."

"Sustained," Judge Tyland agreed. "The jury will disregard the witnesses' last statement."

"Can you just tell us about your findings?" the defense attorney asked.

"Of course. Like I was saying," he started looking at the prosecutor and then at the attorney. "Yvonna never dealt with some of the issues she had in her life so she compensated in other ways. After she murdered her father while taking on Gabriella, the dominate personality, she couldn't deal with the lost and the guilt she felt inside. So after his murder, she took on her father's unstable behavior and identity. She only becomes her father, when she feels the need to be loved or protected."

"Is that why she murdered Bilal? Because she felt she needed protection from him?" Larry asked.

"In a matter of speaking because after learning about Bilal's indiscretion the night of his murder, the father personality took over. Gabriella was used more so if she wanted to commit the murders, but didn't have enough strength to do it alone. Gabriella is by far the most dangerous of the personalities."

"What makes Yvonna's case so extreme," Terrell continued. "Is the fact that sometimes if she battles with what she knows is right, versus what she believes is wrong, the personality will *completely* take over and Yvonna will have no memory of the incident. This is why she doesn't remember killing her father and the victim at Friday's. Gabriella took over on both occasions. It is also important to understand that this condition usually occurs as a result of severe trauma. And since Yvonna recalls being molested while under hypnosis, I'd definitely say she's an excellent candidate for the Multiple Personality Disorder."

"I understand. So do you have something for us to see to support your claims?"

"Yes. And it's very graphic."

A Week Later

"Jury have you reached a verdict?" Judge Tyland asked.

Yvonna looked worried and innocent as she awaited their decision.

"Yes, we the people find Yvonna Harris not guilty by reason of insanity." An older black woman said. The courtroom erupted in noise.

Yvonna hugged her attorney and smiled at Dave who had been supporting her the entire time.

"Order in the court!" Judge Tyland yelled.

The jury was so taken aback by what they saw on the hypnotism tapes, that they felt she didn't deserve jail and needed help. The way she spoke of the rape when she was a child, and how her mother didn't believe her, tugged at their hearts.

The judge immediately sentenced her to time in a psychiatric facility. She was not to be released until deemed fitting by the doctor. The court was in an uproar as Yvonna was whisked away. Her story stayed in the papers for months after the verdict. The headlines read, *A Not So Beautiful Mind.*

~~~~~~

Two years passed and Dave visited her everyday in Green Meadows Psychiatric Facility. After passing numerous evaluations, and continuing her medications, the doctor approved her release.

Bernice and Cream weren't happy about Yvonna getting out either. In fact, they were terrified. Because if she was free, they knew their lives were in danger.

Treyana didn't worry too much because she was happy. She and Avante moved in together and bought a home in Maryland with the twins. So life for her couldn't be better.

And when Yvonna finally walked out of the hospital's doors, Dave was there to greet her. She ran up to him and threw her arms around his body. Lifting her up into the air, he didn't let her go until he finally believed he wasn't dreaming, and that she was actually free.

"You waited for me. You really waited for me." She cried into his arms.

"I love you, Yvonna. I've always loved you from the moment I laid eyes on you. And I want to spend the rest of my life with you."

"And I love you too baby." They engaged into a heated kiss, went home and made love. Three months after her release, they were married.

If you believe in happily ever after
Don't
Turn
The
Page

Reign

Chapter Forty-Two

Complete

"*You know I can't believe we're actually* married," Dave said looking into his wife's eyes, as she lay on top of him. Something about her was different since she'd been home, and he couldn't place his finger on it. But Dave tried to make the best of things, since they were in a beautiful villa in Jamaica away from civilization. They didn't tell a soul they eloped and had flown out of the country.

"Why not?" she questioned kissing him softly on the lips as her breasts pressed against his bare chest.

"Number one...I was always feeling you but you wasn't checkin' for me."

She laughed.

"You think it's funny or something?"

"No, baby," she smiled kissing him again, the breeze from the beautiful Jamaican sky touching their bodies through an open window.

"Then why you laughing?"

"Because I think *you're* funny," she advised looking coldly at him.

"And why is that?"

"Because. You're the reason things worked out the way that they did for me. I could've never done all of this without you."

"What you talkin' 'bout?" he smiled a little worried at her tone.

"I'm talkin' about if it wasn't for you, I would've never been able to get away with all the things I got away with."

He sat up straight in the bed, forcing her to do the same.

"What are you saying Yvonna?"

"Call me Gabriella."

Terror washed over him.

"She's not as strong as I am, so I've decided to take over full time. But don't worry, she'll be around."

"So you're telling me you're Gabriella, and not Yvonna?"

"Of course," she grinned. "But don't look that way honey. She'll be fine. It's just that she was feeling you too much for my taste. Both of you were so much in love it was sickening to watch. At first I was mad at her for going to the doctor's office. And then it dawned on me, if I act as soft as Yvonna and get people to feel sorry for me, perhaps they wouldn't put us away. So right after hypnosis, I decided to take over permanently. And now here we are."

"So what now? You had me marry you on the strength of some bullshit?"

"No. We needed you," she said as she crawled back on top of him, pushing him flat on his back. Her sex appeal still on blast.

Dave was confused, what had he done? And before he could think about it, she removed a knife from up under the pillow and sliced his throat. Silencing him for life. Dave placed both hands on his throat trying to save himself. It didn't work.

"Don't fight it. You'll only make it worse." She pleaded.

She watched him until his breath left his body. She wanted to be the last thing he saw. And when she was sure she was, she got dressed and opened the drawer containing her list. Crossing his name off, she smiled when she realized her work was done. But grabbing a clean sheet of paper she felt it was time for a second Shyt List. And this one would end more violently than the last.

Bernice Santana
Cream Justice
Jhane Jones
Swoopes

"So now what?" Yvonna asked as she appeared by her side.

"We're going to finish what you started. With me in the lead they won't see us coming. You ready for what we have to do?" Gabriella questioned.

"Yes." She smiled.

Folding the piece of paper she tucked it safely inside her pocket, and walked out the door. Alone.

Cartel Publications Order Form
www.thecartelpublications.com
Inmates ONLY get novels for $10.00 per book!

Titles   Fee

Titles		Fee
Shyt List	_____	$15.00
Shyt List 2	_____	$15.00
Pitbulls In A Skirt	_____	$15.00
Pitbulls In A Skirt 2	_____	$15.00
Victoria's Secret	_____	$15.00
Poison	_____	$15.00
Poison 2	_____	$15.00
Hell Razor Honeys	_____	$15.00
Hell Razor Honeys 2	_____	$15.00
A Hustler's Son 2	_____	$15.00
Black And Ugly As Ever	_____	$15.00
Year of The Crack Mom	_____	$15.00
The Face That Launched A Thousand Bullets	_____	$15.00
The Unusual Suspects	_____	$15.00
Miss Wayne & The Queens of DC	_____	$15.00

Please add $2.00 per book for shipping and handling.

The Cartel Publications * P.O. Box 486 * Owings Mills * MD * 21117

Name: _____

Address: _____

City/State: _____

Contact # & Email:

_____

Please allow 5-7 business days for delivery. The Cartel is not responsible for prison orders rejected.